Titles in The Bizarre Baron Inventions

The Magnificent Flying Baron Estate

The Splendid Baron Submarine

The Wonderful Baron Doppelgänger Device

The Tremendous Baron Time Machine

Praise for

The Magnificent Flying Baron Estate

"Kids will want to come along for this action-packed flight as Waldo defines his true character and learns how to be his best self."

—*Story Monsters Ink*

"*The Magnificent Flying Baron Estate* is an enjoyable old-school Western with a contemporary feel . . . kids aged 9–12 are bound to enjoy this topsy-turvy tale with its funny moments of slapstick comedy."

—*The Children's Book Review*

Praise for

The Splendid Baron Submarine

"Delightfully absurd, imaginative, and fun, W. B.'s adventures will make for great read-aloud fare."

—*Foreword Reviews, Starred Review*

"Fans of the first book will be eager to read this sequel."

—*School Library Journal*

THE BIZARRE BARON INVENTIONS

THE TREMENDOUS
BARON TIME MACHINE

Eric Bower

AMBERJACK
PUBLISHING

Idaho

Amberjack Publishing
1472 E. Iron Eagle Dr.
Eagle, Idaho 83616
http://amberjackpublishing.com

Publisher's Cataloging-in-Publication data
Names: Bower, Eric, author.
Title: The tremendous Baron time machine / by Eric Bower.
Description: New York ; Idaho : Amberjack Publishing, [2018] | Series:
Bizarre Baron Inventions ; 4 | Summary: After W.B. discovers a popular
series of books that depict the Barons as bumbling fools, ruining their
reputation and leaving them without an income, P invents a time machine
so W.B. can set things right.
Identifiers: LCCN 2018002156 (print) | LCCN 2018009347 (ebook) | ISBN
9781944995775 (eBook) | ISBN 9781944995782 (hardcover : alk. paper)
Subjects: | CYAC: Time travel--Fiction. | Inventors--Juvenile fiction. |
Family life--Fiction. | Humorous stories.
Classification: LCC PZ7.1.B685 (ebook) | LCC PZ7.1.B685 Tr 2018 (print)
| DDC
[Fic]--dc23
LC record available at https://lccn.loc.gov/2018002156

Cover Design & Illustrations: Agnieszka Grochalska

Printed in the United States of America

For Laura. For everything.

TABLE OF CONTENTS

HE GETS HIS HAIR CUT BY ANGRY SQUIRRELS

JANUARY 9TH, 1892

I couldn't believe my eyes.

Neither could Mr. Cooks, the owner of the Pitchfork bookstore.

"Hey, kid!" he called to me from inside. "Get your eyeballs off my display window! They're smudging up the glass!"

"Sorry."

I ripped my eyes from the display window before flinging open the door and rushing inside the bookstore.

"Where's the latest Sheriff Hoyt Graham adventure novel?" I demanded, pointing to the empty space on the shelf where the Sheriff Hoyt Graham adventure novels could usually be found. "The new shipment was supposed to come in today!"

I guess you could say that I'm a bit of a bookworm—though I wish people would have asked my opinion before they came up with that nickname for readers who really love books. If they had asked me, I would have voted for us to be called "book dragons," or "book wolverines," or even "book anteaters," anything other than *worms*. I have very little in common with worms. Worms are gross. They crawl around in mud, they ruin apples by making them mushy, and you can't tell their heads from their backsides.

Only one of those things is true about me.

Anyway, I'm what you might call a bit of a "book wolverine," so I take my reading very seriously. For the past few years, my favorite books have been novels about the adventures of Sheriff Hoyt Graham, the bravest, smartest, strongest, and most heroic sheriff in history.

The books are loosely based on a real sheriff named Sheriff Hoyt Graham, who is the sheriff here in the Wild West town of Pitchfork, Arizona Territory. The real Sheriff Graham was a nice old man, but he wasn't much of a law officer. He never stopped robberies, or caught bandits, or won gunfights. And he wasn't particularly strong.

In fact, he was so weak that he often needed help bringing his soup spoon to his mouth if the spoon held anything heavier than a pea. And as far as intelligence was concerned, it was fair to say that he wasn't the shiniest fork in the sink, if you know what I mean. There was a family of skunks living under his house that frequently outsmarted him. It wasn't unusual here in Pitchfork to see a family of skunks run down Main Street, dressed in a law officer's clothing, with a furious Sheriff Hoyt Graham dressed in his holey long johns running after them while shaking his tiny fist.

But other than that, Sheriff Graham was practically identical to the sheriff in the books.

Mr. Cooks rolled his eyes and snorted at me, as though I had just said the daftest thing he'd ever heard.

"Sheriff Hoyt Graham books?" he asked snidely. "Nobody reads those anymore, kid. Those books are duller than ice water soup." He reached behind the counter and picked up a large box of books, which he emptied onto the countertop. "This is what everyone is reading nowadays. You're lucky I just got a new shipment in this morning. They've been selling out every day."

I looked at the cover of one of the books, and for the second time that morning, I couldn't believe my eyes.

I gasped in shock, though to tell you the truth, I'm not a very good gasper, so the noise that came out of my mouth just sounded like a normal breath. Since I couldn't properly express my surprise through gasping, I had to do the opposite of a gasp, which, after a moment of thought, I decided was a sneeze.

I sneezed in shock.

"If you sneeze on a book, then that means you've bought it," Mr. Cooks warned. "These books are more popular than those silly sheriff stories ever were. And they're much more entertaining. I nearly busted a gut reading the last one!"

He picked up one of the books and handed it to me. I slowly read the title on the cover out loud.

"*The Hilarious Mis-Adventures of the Ridiculous Baron Family.*"

The cover illustration showed a wild haired inventor with crazy eyes, along with his stern and serious looking

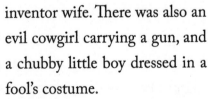

inventor wife. There was also an evil cowgirl carrying a gun, and a chubby little boy dressed in a fool's costume.

All four of them were hanging from the balcony of a

vaguely familiar flying home, which puttered across the sky in the middle of a wacky race around the country.

Mr. Cooks looked from my face, to the cover of the book, and then back to my face again.

"Say," he said as he scratched his chin, "you and the chubby fool on the cover look like you could be twins!"

There's a very good reason why the fool on the cover and I looked identical to one another—except, of course, for the fool's costume. Although, come to think of it, I *did* used to own a pair of pajamas that looked a bit like that costume, due to the multicolored patches that were sewn all over it. And the jingly bells sewn into the neckline. And then there was the rather unfortunate sleeping hat (which was also adorned with several jingly bells, and had the word "FOOL" stitched across the front).

The drawing of the fool on the cover of the book *was* actually a drawing of me. The family on the cover was my family. We are the ridiculous Baron family. Though we prefer just to be called the Baron family.

Let me try to explain this as quickly as I can . . .

My name is Waldo Baron, but since I'd rather be shot out of a cannon and into a briar patch than hear anyone call me that, I prefer to go by the name W. B. I'm eleven years old. My parents, Sharon and McLaron Baron (whom I call M and P, instead of Ma and Pa), are two of the cleverest inventors who have ever lived. In the past year, they've invented a winged flying machine, a Shrinking Machine, a Bigging Machine, a coal powered submarine, a rocket, and a device that can transform you into someone else with the simple press of a button. They also transformed our home into a giant flying machine, which we used to participate in a race around the country. We didn't win the race, but we still had a marvelous time.

My parents have invented many other fantastic things as well, but unfortunately, I can't really remember any of those inventions right now. Sorry. And in case you're wondering, I have no idea how any of my parents' inventions work, so please don't ask me to explain them to you. I know even less about science and mathematics than I know about . . . actually, I can't think of *anything* I know less about than science and mathematics. Maybe Japanese tea ceremonies. But that's about it.

We live in a large house on the outskirts of Pitchfork, and our property is called the Baron Estate. Also living with us at the Baron Estate is my parents' trusty assistant, a woman by the name of Rose Blackwood. Rose is a former villain (who once tried to kidnap my family), and her older brother is Benedict Blackwood, who is the worst criminal in the world. But Rose was never really evil to begin with, even when she was trying to be a villain. She was probably the politest kidnapper you could imagine—always apologizing whenever she had to threaten our lives. My parents hired her to be their assistant, a job she absolutely loves. And she's quite good at it too. Rose is engaged to Deputy Buddy Graham, who is Sheriff Hoyt Graham's son. Their wedding is in a couple of weeks, and everyone is really excited about it.

There's another person who lives with us in the Baron Estate, but I'm currently quite mad at her, so I won't mention her by name unless I absolutely must.

Because of my parents' inventions and experiments, we've had a lot of wild adventures. Those adventures are pretty well known to most of the people in Arizona Territory. In fact, I've heard that our adventures are pretty well known to people all over the country. I've never thought of us as national heroes or anything (though we did find a lost treasure a few months ago, and returned it to its rightful owners instead of keeping it for ourselves), but I've certainly never considered us to be a national joke.

Which is how we all looked on the cover of these new adventure books. Like a big, fat joke.

"Wait a minute," Mr. Cooks said as he snapped his fingers. "Your last name is Baron, too, isn't it? And your parents are both inventors. Zow-wee! These books are about you, kid! Hah!"

There were several other people in the bookstore who looked over at me. Each one of them had the new Baron book in their hands. They looked from the book cover, to my face, and then back to the book cover again. Then, after looking at the cover and my face a few more times to be certain (people aren't very clever here in Pitchfork), they started to laugh.

"He's right! It *is* about the Baron family!" hooted one of them.

"Look, they even got little Waldo's funny haircut right on the cover!" another one jeered.

I looked in the window and stared at my reflection. Why did people always make comments about my haircut? Had they not noticed my father's hair? P had a terrible habit of being struck by lightning, and every time it happened, his hair turned a shade whiter and stood up in porcupine spikes. Because of that, he had the most ridiculous hairstyle this side of the Mississippi. And yet people always made fun of mine. Why? Why I ask you?

As several new people poured into the bookstore, people like Miss Danielle (my school teacher), Mr. Thornberry (the mayor of Pitchfork), Mr. Dadant (the town beekeeper), Mrs. Pyramus (the town weaver), and Madge Tweetie (one of my least favorite people in town, who also happened to be the best friend of . . . the person I'm refusing to mention), they each grabbed copies of the latest Baron book.

Mr. Cooks was right. The Baron books were clearly the most popular books in the shop. They were selling like two cent hotcakes with a free side of bacon.

. . .

. . .

. . . I'm sorry, I just distracted myself for a moment with thoughts of bacon. Back to the story.

"I can't believe we never knew how funny the Barons were!" Mrs. Pyramus exclaimed as she started the first chapter.

"Wait until you get to the part about little Waldo losing his pants while hanging out of his bedroom window!" Mr. Cooks chortled.

"Hey, I lost my pants while I was hanging out of *my aunt's* bedroom window!" I angrily corrected him. But no one bothered to listen to me.

They were all too busy laughing.

"What a load of gullyfluff!" Madge Tweetie hooted, laughing so hard that she dropped her book and nearly toppled over. "The Barons are a bunch of bull-goose fools! I always knew they were goofy, but I didn't know they were actual buffoons!"

I knew for a fact that Madge Tweetie often mis-spelled her own name, and yet *she* was calling *us* buffoons? Sure, my family and I would occasionally have little *mis-steps* during our adventures. Sometimes things wouldn't go exactly as planned. But we had still done some pretty impressive things, things that no one else in the world could do. It made me angry that these people would dismiss us as fools. After all, my parents were two of the most brilliant inventors who had ever lived! And Rose Blackwood was also quite clever and remarkably brave! And I . . . well . . . my haircut wasn't that bad!

But that didn't stop the people from mocking us.

"He sure does fall down and hit his head a lot in this book," commented Mr. Dadant as he glanced at me with a frown. "I'm amazed that Waldo hasn't suffered any permanent brain damage."

"We don't know for certain that he hasn't," my teacher Miss Danielle muttered, turning a page in her book.

"Hah! At the end of this chapter, Waldo is almost crushed by wild pigs!" Mrs. Pyramus cried out with a giggle.

"What a hilarious story!"

"Has McLaron Baron *really* been struck by lightning over twenty times?"

"Rose Blackwood was *seriously* fooled into believing that Waldo was his own aunt, just because he dressed up in one of her frilly nightgowns?"

"The Barons *actually* have a family happy dance that they do when they're excited? How odd!"

"They really are ridiculous, aren't they?"

"I can't believe I used to admire them!"

"I can't believe I used to be impressed with their inventions

and adventures."

"I can't believe I used to tell my children to study hard in school, so they could be like the Barons when they grew up. Who would want to be like them?"

"I was never impressed by the Barons. In fact, they deserve to have a ridiculous book written about them. Only foozlers, dalcops, scobberlotchers, dew-beaters, and vulgar nincompoops appear in books!" Madge Tweetie declared, as she turned another page with a frown on her face. "Well, how do you like this? My stupid best friend is one of the main characters in this book, and she hasn't even mentioned me once . . ."

Soon, the entire book store was filled with nasty laughter, laughter directed at me and my parents and Rose Blackwood. With my cheeks burning bright red from shame, I reached into my pocket, and dropped a few cents onto Mr. Cooks's counter. I grabbed my copy of *The Hilarious Mis-Adventures of the Ridiculous Baron Family*, and ran out of the store as quickly as I could.

I paused to catch my breath. My heart was thundering,

my legs ached, my throat burned, my lungs felt like they were deflating, and my spleen felt a little swimmy.

I'd been running for about six seconds.

Alright, I'm not what you would call a "runner." Or a "jogger." Or even a "fast walker." I'm more of a "sitter," and a "lay-downer," and a "hides-in-the-closet-so-I-won't-be-forced-to-go-anywhere-or-do-anything-er." My body doesn't enjoy running, and since upsetting my body usually leads to my body upsetting me right back, I don't often push it.

When I had finally caught my breath, I gingerly walked the rest of the way across our dusty, little western town then down the long and winding road running through the Pitchfork Desert. It was the only road leading to the Baron Estate.

The Baron Estate is the only home I've ever known, and I can't imagine growing up in a better place. Sure, we're all alone in the middle of a dry and quiet desert with no neighbors around us for miles—except for the coyotes, snakes, lizards, vultures, and scorpions, all of whom are a lot less friendly than you might think. But M is an ingenious chemist who used her talent for mixing things in beakers to come up with a special, secret chemical that allows us to grow a lush and lovely garden in the middle of the desert. Even though the land surrounding us is dead and dry, our property is covered with green grass, lovely flowers, and fruit trees all year long. Our property is always much greener than the rest of Pitchfork, which I suppose has made the townspeople resent us a bit. Whenever we go into town, they all start bragging about their dirt farms, and telling us how no one with any brains bothers to eat gross things like oranges and cherries anymore.

The Baron Estate is a two-story house with a work garage attached, which is where M and P typically build their inventions. We also have a little barn in the backyard where we keep our horse, Geoffrey. There is extra room in the barn for some of my parents' larger inventions, like their horseless carriage, which is exactly what it sounds like—a carriage that moves without horses.

I've recently heard that our horseless carriage has inspired a lot of other inventors in the country to try and build horseless carriages of their own, but I doubt they'll be successful. I wouldn't be surprised if my parents' invention was the only successful horseless carriage ever built. Take it from me, W. B., when I say that you'll never have to worry about a bunch of horseless carriages clogging up the roads.

I crossed the final desert hump and spotted the white picket fence surrounding my family home. I looked at the cover of *The Hilarious Mis-Adventures of the Ridiculous Baron Family*, and then back at our house. It wasn't just my family that was being portrayed poorly by the book. Our house was being portrayed poorly as well. The illustration on the cover showed a tall and rickety shack with peeling paint, rotting floorboards, and a cracked chimney that looked as though it was slowly trying to tiptoe off the rooftop. It was nothing like the real Baron Estate, which was always in tiptop shape. For some reason, that made me madder than anything. You should never insult anyone or anything that can't defend itself. Like a house. Or a tree. Or a cow. Or Mr. Bessie, the crazy, old local grocer, who for some reason always calls me "Julia." It's just not right.

Shivering lightly from the wintertime chill, I ran up the front steps (stopping a couple times to catch my breath), tore open the door, and rushed inside.

"OWWWWWWWW!" Rose Blackwood bellowed.

"Sorry, Rose," said P, "but I warned you not to move."

Rose glared at me.

"I wouldn't have moved," she told him, "if W. B. hadn't

dashed into the living room like a wild animal and startled me!"

"I'm not a wild animal!" I growled (but in the way that a human growls, not a wild animal). "I just wanted you all to know that someone has been wr—*what on earth are you wearing, Rose?*"

Rose's cheeks turned as red as the rose she normally wore in the band of her hat. She was standing on a footstool in the living room dressed in an incredibly long and poofy white dress. It was the fanciest thing I'd ever seen her wear, the sort of thing you'd expect to see worn by royalty or by a dead person.

If you knew Rose like I did, then you'd know that seeing her wearing a fancy white dress was sort of like seeing a gorilla . . . which was also wearing a fancy white dress. She rarely wore anything other than her black hat, black shirt, black pants, and red boots. She once told me that she had nothing against dresses, but she also had nothing against badgers, and she wouldn't want to wear one of them either.

"Hold still, Rose," P ordered. "I haven't finished this seam yet."

My father had about a half-dozen pins clutched tightly between his teeth. He had a tailor's measuring tape wrapped over his shoulders like a scarf, and he was carefully sewing a long strip of see-through material (which looked sort of like a tail made of spider webs) to Rose's backside.

"What's that?" I asked, pointing to the see-through fabric.

"That's the train!" P stated proudly. Rose nodded excitedly.

I was confused. I must have heard him incorrectly.

"Train? Like, *choo-choo, all aboard,* train? I don't understand how you could use that as a train, unless of course all the train passengers were the size of fleas. Which you probably wouldn't want to have on your backside in the first place."

"It's the train for my wedding dress, you chowderhead," Rose said as she rolled her eyes. "Mr. Baron was kind enough to sew my wedding dress for me. You do know what a wedding dress is, don't you?"

I rolled my eyes back at her even harder, which was a mistake, because it sort of hurt.

"*Of course* I know what a wedding dress is. I just don't understand why it needs a locomotive attached to it."

P finished his final stitch before turning to me.

"We aren't talking about locomotives, son. A train on

a wedding dress is the material attached to the back of the dress that trails behind the bride as she walks down the aisle."

"That's right," Rose said with a nod.

P continued his explanation.

"The purpose of the train is to make the bride look like a ghost that's hovering across the floor, haunting the wedding ceremony. You can't have a wedding without a person dressed like a ghost. It's just not right. It's a tradition. How do you not know any of this, W. B.?"

"What? Who told you that?" Rose asked P. "That's the most ridiculous thing I've ever heard."

"Of course I knew that," I lied to P, not wanting to look like an ignorant fool on the subject of weddings. "I was just kidding. Everyone knows that brides are supposed to look like ghosts. That's why they have veils that cover their faces. It makes them look extra frightening."

"But that's not true—" Rose started to interrupt.

"Quite right, son," P said with a nod of his pointy head. "That's why it's bad luck for the groom to see the bride in her wedding dress before the wedding. He might mistake her for an actual ghost and run away screaming."

"You two have no idea what you're talking about," Rose groaned.

"That's also why there are usually two or three men standing next to the groom during the wedding ceremony, isn't it?" I said to P. "They're there to keep the groom from running away in case he gets scared of the ghost."

"I'm leaving," Rose muttered. She hopped off the stool and made her way to the kitchen, slowly shaking her head, and mumbling to herself.

"Correct," P told me as he patted me on the shoulder. "That's why at the beginning of the ceremony, the first thing the groom should do is lift the veil from the bride's face to make sure that she's not *really* a ghost. You can never be too careful about that. I've heard several cases of a groom waiting until after the wedding to lift their bride's veils, only to find that he's been married to a horrible demon instead."

"Weddings are pretty spooky, aren't they, P?"

"Yes, son. Yes, they are."

I called a family meeting to discuss what I'd discovered at the bookstore that morning. Everyone gathered in the kitchen. Normally, we gathered in my parents' work garage for our family meetings, but I told them to gather in the kitchen instead because I was hungry.

While I explained to them how we had become the punchline to Pitchfork's newest and cruelest joke, I snacked on the leftovers from last night's supper. There actually weren't too many leftovers left, since last night I'd had four servings of the hearty stew, sweet potatoes, buttered peas, and the blackberry crumble that P had prepared. So, when I finished what was left of the leftovers, I made myself a few ham and cheese sandwiches to tide me over until supper, or at least until my next snack.

Being angry tends to make me hungry. I also get a bit snackish when I'm sad. And a little peckish when I'm happy. And a bit tummy-rumbly when I'm in a silly mood. And I get absolutely ravenous when I'm frightened or confused or tired or bored or concerned or thoughtful or bitter or enthusiastic or anxious or weary or stressed or uncomfortable or comfortable. I suppose the only time I'm not really hungry is when I'm asleep, though I've had enough donut-based dreams to know that this might not be the case.

"So as you can see," I told them with my mouth full of cheese, while gesturing to the terrible book that M, P, and Rose were slowly thumbing through, "we clearly need to do something about these terrible books. Otherwise, the good Baron family name will be ruined, forever *besmirched* by these ridiculous rumors that we are loony, evil, clumsy, and eat far more cheese than we should."

I belched into my fist and stumbled, bonking my head against the kitchen cabinet.

Alright. If I'm being perfectly honest with you, I should mention that I'm a bit of a klutz. So, I suppose the writer got that part of the book correct. But the rest of it was utter nonsense.

I belched again.

I'm not quite sure how I expected my family to respond to the news that we were being openly mocked by everyone in town, but I certainly didn't expect them to do what they did next. It started with M, who tilted her head back and closed her eyes. She pinched the bridge of her nose and her shoulders began to shake.

"Please don't cry, M," I told her, quickly finishing the last of my sandwiches, as well as the six cookies I was holding, so I could give her a reassuring hug and a pat on the back. "It'll be alright. I promise. We'll figure out what to do."

But as I crossed the room, I was shocked to find that she wasn't actually crying.

She was laughing. Uproariously! My mother was laughing as hard as she could, as though it was some *other* mother's kid on the cover of the book with a pathetic and frightened look on his chubby face, dressed in brightly colored patchwork clothes, his shoelaces dangling loosely because he wasn't clever enough to tie them, and with a haircut so awful that it looked as though it had been given to him by a blind enemy with shaky hands and dull scissors.

"You're laughing!" I accused. She tried to deny it, but she couldn't. She was laughing too hard.

And since laughter is contagious, it spread to Rose Blackwood next, who read a passage in one of the chapters which tickled her so tremendously that she started to snort with laughter. And since she was terribly embarrassed by her snorts, the snorts were interrupted by silly little giggles that turned her cheeks pink. Rose snorted and giggled pinkly until she looked as though she was about to burst.

Then my father began to laugh in long, loud guffaws. My father is a very strange man, so it only made sense that he had a very strange laugh as well. Most strange people have strange laughs. I don't know why. But it's true. P's laughter sounded like someone bouncing up and down on a giant accordion. It was a loud blasting sound, followed by the shrill hiss of him taking in a deep breath, in order to make another loud blast. As he laughed, he slapped the table so hard that I thought he might chop it in half.

Every time it seemed as though they would finally stop their ridiculous bout of uncontrollable laughter, they would glance at one another and start again. It was madness. From outside, I could hear Geoffrey the horse whinnying and braying with laughter as well, which I thought was pretty stupid, since he obviously had no idea what was going on. There was no way he could have read the book cover from all the way out there.

It seemed as though everyone in the Baron Estate found the book to be pretty darn funny, except for me . . . and except for one other person as well.

Oh, crumbs.

I suppose I'll have to mention her, even though I really don't want to. Just remember, I'm not very happy with her at the moment. You'll find out why soon.

As Rose and my parents continued laughing their clever heads off in the kitchen, a woman with a permanent frown painted on her face waddled in. She was wearing one of her old fashioned high-necked dresses, with puffy sleeves and ruffles down the front. Her hair was piled on top of her head like a hastily packed picnic lunch. Her face was a very unique color, a color that can best be described as "zorple." And I dare you to look at her without thinking of an egg. Go on. Try it. You can't, can you? I told you so.

"What's going on here?" my eggy Aunt Dorcas demanded. "You're all cackling like a bunch of flatulent hyenas!"

And then she happened to notice the copy of *The Hilarious Mis-Adventures of the Ridiculous Baron Family* lying on the table.

She picked it up and stared at the cover.

"Not bad," she said with a nod, "but the artist didn't get W. B.'s hairstyle right. In the illustration, it simply looks like someone attacked him with hedge clippers. In real life, he looks as though he gets his hair cut by angry squirrels."

LIKE A SNEEZE IN THE WIND

Once Rose stopped giggling and snorting, she explained to Aunt Dorcas what the book was about, and how it painted us as brainless jesters whose adventures were nothing more than accidents and embarrassing mishaps. Aunt Dorcas remained silent as Rose spoke, but her eyes grew smaller and smaller as they squinted in anger, until it looked as though they had completely disappeared from her face.

"And you're all laughing about this?" she asked quietly when Rose had finished.

"Well, W. B. isn't," M said, removing her wire-rimmed eyeglasses and cleaning them with her handkerchief. "He needs to learn not to take himself so seriously. Otherwise, he could end up like—"

I could see M's mouth start to say the name "Dorcas," before she noticed the ugly look on her zorple-faced sister's countenance. My mother quickly coughed into her fist before changing the subject.

"Why didn't you buy one of your Sheriff Graham novels instead, W. B.?" M asked.

"Because no one reads those novels anymore!" I told her. "They're all too busy reading stories about us! Terrible stories, stories that make us look dumber than a box of string! String!"

"I don't understand why you're so upset about this, W. B.," Rose told me as she mussed up my already mussy hair. "I honestly think the whole thing is pretty funny. Who cares if people laugh at us? They're just silly books. They can't do us any harm. In fact, I'd be willing to bet that no one will even remember them in a few weeks."

But that's where Rose was very, very wrong.

"What do you mean, *you're no longer interested in buying our inventions?*"

Mr. Pyles nervously fiddled with his tie and then with

his glasses. He was the most nervous and fiddly person I'd ever met. Mr. Pyles was always nervously fiddling with something or other: his tie, his glasses, his hair, his collar, his sleeve, his nose, his ears, your ears, the strange little wart growing out of his chin. He was a man who was utterly uncomfortable in his skin and felt the constant need to fiddle. It almost seemed as though he was worried he might explode if he didn't constantly fiddle, fiddle, fiddle. I once asked him if he had any relaxing hobbies outside of work. He nervously explained to me that he liked to go home and play the fiddle.

I should have seen that answer coming.

But as nervous and fiddly as he was, Mr. Pyles was very important to us, because he was one of the business-men in Pitchfork who paid my parents for their inventions. Most of M and P's fantastic inventions (like their flying machines and submarine) were too strange, terrifying, and expensive for Mr. Pyles's taste, but he was always excited to learn when my parents had invented a new automatic butter-smearer, or a hat that washes your hair for you. And he would pay good money for those inventions. My parents often joked that Mr. Pyles was only interested in useless and silly gadgets, ignoring their impressive and significant inventions because he was afraid of anything he couldn't understand. But it appeared that he wasn't interested in anything anymore. At least, not anything that had been invented by someone named Baron.

In fact, *no one* was interested in my parents' inventions anymore. The previous day, the other local businessmen who bought inventions from my parents had come by the Baron Estate to tell us that they were no longer interested in purchasing any inventions, though they wished my parents good luck in the future. In fact, they all made quite a big show about wishing them good luck, as though it was the greatest gift they could give.

I don't know about you, but my family needs money to survive, not luck. Luck won't buy you a ham sandwich. Neither will well wishes, words of sympathy, respectful head nods, polite pats on the shoulder, and tickle-fights. The man at the Pitchfork sandwich shop had made that quite clear to me.

But that's all anyone was giving us: well wishes that didn't seem particularly sincere.

"I mean . . ." Mr. Pyles stammered, as he fidgeted and fiddled with his eyelids, ". . . times being what they are . . . I mean, since I don't really need . . . uh, I mean, you see . . . inventions are no longer . . . uh, I mean . . . the ostrich is a funny bird . . ."

"Oh, stop your fiddling and just tell me the truth!" M snapped at Mr. Pyles in a very rare moment of losing her temper. "You no longer want to do business with us because of those stupid books. Just admit it. You think we're fools now, just like everyone else!"

Mr. Pyles began to nervously fiddle and fidget so much that he actually started to look like a blur. It was as though my mother was talking to a smudge at the kitchen door instead of a person.

"I mean . . . perhaps that might be . . . one of many reasons . . . but . . . you see . . . eucalyptus . . . and . . . wishing you luck . . . best of . . . sympathy . . . and wishing wells . . ."

My mother shut the door in his face. There was only so much fiddling and fidgeting you can stand to watch before it starts to make you a little seasick.

"Well, that was our last buyer," Rose said glumly. "What are we going to do now?"

"I'm not quite certain," M replied with a helpless shrug. "I suppose we'll have to reach out to new people who might want to purchase our inventions. We could travel across Arizona Territory and sell some of our smaller inventions door-to-door. We could visit county fairs and give demonstrations. Or maybe we can try to sell some of our larger and more expensive inventions to the government. They always show quite a bit of interest in our large inventions, even if we don't necessarily approve of the ways that they'd like to use them."

Though she tried to keep a smile on her face, M didn't sound particularly excited about any of that. She turned to my father, who was seated at the kitchen table, and reading *The Hilarious Mis-Adventures of the Ridiculous Baron Family*. He'd been reading it quite a lot lately, though he no longer appeared to find it particularly funny. In fact, the expression on his face was as serious an expression as I'd ever seen my father wear. It reminded me of how he looked when he had completed roughly seventy-five percent of a brilliant thought or idea, usually pertaining to an invention that made absolutely no sense to yours truly. In fact, he was so distracted by the book, he hadn't even bothered to sew his horse a new winter hat.

P has a strange thing about hats. For some reason, it's very important to him that our animals have appropriate new hats for each and every season. Yes, you read that correctly. *Our animals.*

I've been forced to wear the same winter hat for four years now. It's as thin and holey as an abandoned cobweb, and provides my head with all the warmth and protection of a used handkerchief. P has been promising to buy or sew me a new hat for about three years now, but that promise always seems to fly out the window whenever he decides that our horse's head looks a bit chilly or it doesn't look stylish enough.

Though I must admit, it could be worse. He's been promising my mother that he'll repair the scraggly head of our old kitchen mop for about six years now. And he's yet to even start on that.

So, that's where I rank in the Baron house. Just below the family horse, and just above the mop.

"McLaron?" my mother said. "What do you think we should do?"

"Hmmm, wow, yes, of course, right, that sounds good to me, my little muffin," P muttered absently, clearly not listening to a word that M was saying. "Or bad. Or neither. Or both. Whatever you like, dear. You know best."

"McLaron!"

P dropped his book and looked up at my mother in shock, like he'd just been shaken awake from an intense dream.

"Yes, my little muffin?" he said. "Wait, where did Mr.

Pyles go? I have his new mechanical hairbrush in the work garage. And unlike the last one, this one won't burrow into his hair like a frightened gopher."

"He's not interested in buying the mechanical hairbrush from us," Rose told him. "He's not interested in buying *anything* from us ever again. It's because of those stupid books! No one wants an invention made by the Barons because they're afraid that something will be wrong with them. The books have completely ruined our reputation. W. B. was right."

"What was that?" I said, pointing to my ear. "I don't think I heard you correctly. Who was right? Some clever young fellow with initials for a name? Why, he must be the smartest kid in the whole world."

"Be quiet, W. B., this is serious."

"She's right," said M, as she picked up the latest copy of the local newspaper, *The Pitchfork Pitchfork* (I know it's not a very good name, but there aren't a lot of creative people living in Pitchfork). "Look at the cover story. Our books are not only the bestselling books in Arizona Territory, they're also the bestselling books on the West Coast. Soon, the entire country will be reading them."

"And then no one in America will trust our inventions," Rose sighed, "which will be quite a big problem for me.

My wedding is only a week away, and I could really use the money to help pay for it. It turns out that weddings are really expensive."

"Maybe Buddy could pay for the wedding?" I suggested.

Rose shook her head.

"First of all, it's tradition for the family of the bride to pay for the wedding. My parents are rich bank robbers who could afford to throw me a huge wedding, but they still haven't forgiven me for helping to send my brother Benedict to jail twice. Not to mention the fact that they'd be terribly disappointed that I'm marrying an honest deputy instead of a dastardly bank robber or odious horse thief. Secondly, Buddy doesn't have two dimes to rub together. He's broke. His father doesn't pay him very much to work as a deputy, and most of the money he's made recently has gone toward repairing the clock tower in the center of town."

"Why?" M asked. "What happened to the clock?"

"Buddy accidentally shot the hands off it when he fell off his horse while sneezing. The mayor is forcing him to pay for it."

I felt bad for Buddy. That's the sort of thing that would usually happen to me. In fact, it happened to me last month. Except instead of falling off a horse, I fell off a sheep. And instead of a sneeze, it was a loud hiccup. And instead of a gun, it was a squishy banana. And instead of a clock tower, it was someone's grandmother. But other than that, it was pretty much the same thing.

"You aren't the only one who needs money, Rose," M said quietly. "We're pretty low on funds as well. Last week, we had to buy a large batch of coal to power one of our new inventions. Coal is getting more expensive, which means we had to use a lot of our savings to pay for it. And yesterday, McLaron had to spend quite a bit of money on new shoes and pants for W. B., who appears to be hitting a major growth spurt at a very unfortunate time."

She was right. Last January, I was looking up at everyone as though they were giants. Now, I was almost the same height as Rose and my mother, and I was only a few inches shorter than P. Actually, I was still about a foot or two shorter than P, if you counted his tall and spiky hair. But the point was, I was really starting to grow. I felt rather guilty about growing so much, forcing my parents to spend all that money on new boots and pants while we were having terrible money problems. I quietly told myself to stop growing as I took another bite of my third sausage, cheese, onion, and hot pepper sandwich.

We all sat there silently, wondering if we would have to

do what M had said—travel across the country selling my parents' inventions door to door. That wouldn't be the worst thing in the world, I supposed. In fact, it might be fun. It would allow us to see some more of the country, and meet new people, and have new adventures, and taste new sandwiches. But it would also mean that we'd never be home. We'd be living out of suitcases, spending our nights in dirty hotels and loud saloons, always feeling dirty and grimy, never feeling comfortable. There might be nights when we'd have to sleep in the horseless carriage.

And then there was another unpleasant thought that kept passing through my mind: if we were running out of money, did that mean we'd have to sell the Baron Estate?

It seemed as though we had been hit by a terrible string of bad luck, and we couldn't understand why. After all, we were nice people. We treated everyone kindly. We didn't lie or cheat or steal. We didn't litter or cuss or make fun of people with bad haircuts (which is more than I can say for most people here in Pitchfork . . .). What had we done to deserve this? And more importantly, when would our string of bad luck finally come to an end?

As we sat and wondered, there was a knock at the front door.

Since Rose and my mother were still staring sadly at the newspaper article about the popular Baron books, and my father was still studying his copy of *The Hilarious Mis-Adventures of the Ridiculous Baron Family* as though there was some secret to be unlocked within the pages, I answered the door.

It was Deputy Buddy Graham. Buddy was a tall and gangly man with a wild and curly mop of red hair. He was a bit of a goon, but he was also a very kind person. And since Rose was fond of him, the rest of us were fond of him too. He was a better peace officer than his father, though that wasn't saying much. A sturdy coat rack was probably a better peace officer than Sheriff Hoyt Graham.

Buddy slowly removed his deputy cap as he said hello to me in a somber voice then asked if Rose was home. I couldn't recall ever seeing Buddy look so sad and serious before. Normally he was as happy-go-lucky as a dog in a sausage factory. But at that moment he looked so upset that I began to feel a bit depressed just from looking at him, which of course meant that I started feeling a bit snackish (and for some reason I was suddenly craving another sausage). I invited Buddy inside, but he lingered in the doorway, like he was too sad to set foot inside the Baron Estate.

"Buddy?" Rose called from behind me, her frown quickly twitching into a relieved smile as she walked into the living room. "I can't tell you how glad I am to see you. This has been a horrible day."

Buddy started to speak, but then he bit his lip and quickly turned around. He peered into a cluster of dwarf apple trees in our fruit garden, which appeared to be concealing someone who was trying his best to remain hidden. I could hear that hidden person whispering furiously to Buddy, though I couldn't see who it was or hear what they were saying. Whoever the person was, they appeared to be upsetting Buddy, since the lanky deputy was furiously whispering right back at them. When they had finished furiously whispering to one another, Deputy Buddy turned back to Rose.

"Rose," he said in a voice that cracked, "you look . . . you look absolutely beautiful today."

"Really?" I said, looking at Rose, who was dressed in paint stained clothing. We'd been painting the barn earlier that morning, and some of the paint had gotten onto her hands and arms, as well as in her hair, and in one of her ears too. There was even a blotch of paint at the tip of her nose, which made her look like a clown. "You think so, Buddy? She looks pretty awful to me. All paint-spattered. And she smells a bit ripe, too, from working so hard. But that's Rose. Always sweating. She's definitely a sweater. You can tell she's a sweater by the big sweat stains under the armpits of her work shirt. See the stains? Do you see them? Buddy? The stains?"

"W. B., go away!" Deputy Buddy and Rose both snapped at me at the same time.

Wow. Some people can be rather rude.

I returned to the kitchen where my mother was flipping carefully through the newspaper, just in case there was an ad placed by someone in town looking for new and fantastic inventions that she had missed during her last search of the paper. P still had his nose buried in the Baron book. I couldn't understand why. My father was a genius, and the Baron books were all so poorly written. In my opinion, they weren't funny or clever or creative or even that interesting. Plus, they were just plain embarrassing. Why would he bother reading those stories over and over again? What was the point? My curiosity finally got the best of me, and I asked him about it, knowing very well that his answer would likely be confusing and weird.

"Why are you still looking at that book, P?" I asked. "It's probably the worst thing I've ever read. It's even worse than that book about the female squirrel with the boy's name who stole and hid an antique necklace. What was it called again? *Earl the Girl Squirrel's Squirreled Pearl?* Wait . . . is that an actual book, or is that just from a weird dream I had?"

"Shush, W. B.," P said as he turned another page. "I've found something quite interesting here."

"Nothing," M sighed, setting down the newspaper. "Absolutely nothing. There aren't any new people looking for inventions or devices or even doodads. It looks like we'll have to move. We might even need to start a new line of business and get different jobs. Maybe we could become professors at a college? No, that would never work. Our silly reputation as bumbling fools has probably ruined that for us as well. No one wants to be taught by clowns."

"They would at a *Clown College,*" I said, my brain beginning to dance with the beginnings of a brilliant idea. "You and P could open up the first Clown College in the country! You'd make a ton of money! Plus, it would be a lot of fun. I know I'd rather go to Clown College than to the Pitchfork School. You could teach classes on the best way to juggle fire, do cartwheels, swallow swords, and dance with baby bears dressed in pink skirts! This is a great idea!"

"W. B.," my mother groaned. "You're not helping. Please be quiet."

"Yes, be quiet, W. B.," my father muttered.

Everyone was apparently in very a rude mood.

It was their loss, though. My Clown College idea would make someone very rich one day. Very rich. Stinkin' rich. Stinkin' clown rich, even.

Suddenly we heard shouting from the living room, followed by the sound of our front door slamming closed. A pair of familiar footsteps raced across the living room and into Rose's bedroom, and then another door slammed shut. We could hear the faint sound of Rose weeping.

Aunt Dorcas waddled into the kitchen, slowly shaking her head.

"Well," she said, "I guess we won't have to worry about a wedding now. It's probably for the best. Most of the people who'd already agreed to attend the wedding have recently canceled, including my EX best friend, Madge Tweetie. Hmmph. *Madge*. I curse that horrible woman. May all her pies be sour, and may her ankles grow as wide as the Mississippi!"

"Oh no," said M. "Did Buddy and Rose really end their engagement?"

"Naturally," Aunt Dorcas replied as she reached into the ice box and pulled out a hardboiled egg. "His father wouldn't approve of his only son marrying a foolish villain. And those silly Baron books make Rose look like the world's most foolish villain. Sheriff Graham felt he had no choice but to force his son to call off the wedding. He told Buddy that he'd be fired, disinherited, and disowned if he married Rose, plus he'd be forced to give back his deputy hat, which is the only thing that keeps Buddy Graham from looking like a first-class fool. Under that hat, his head is so pointy that neighborhood kids often mistake it for a ring-toss game."

"Fascinating . . ." my father said quietly, and he turned another page in the book.

"That's terrible news," I said. "Poor Rose."

"Yes, poor Rose indeed," M answered with a sigh. "McLaron, what is so interesting about that book? You haven't put it down in weeks. You must have already read the silly thing cover to cover at least a dozen times."

P put down the book and smiled a strange smile.

Actually, it was just one of his regular smiles, though

it still looked pretty strange. Remember what I said about strange people having strange laughs? It goes double for their smiles. When my father smiled, he looked a bit like a seasick ferret. Or like an owl with a bad taste in its mouth. Or like some other animal with a personal problem.

"You're right, my little muffin," he said to M. "I *should* have this book memorized by now. But I don't. Do you know why?"

"Because you have more important things to do with your time than memorize a stupid book?" I suggested. "Like making certain that your poor, hungry family doesn't starve to death because they've run out of money? Particularly your loving son? Who's already quite hungry?"

"Nope!" P declared, opening the book to what appeared to be a random page and holding it up. "I don't have it memorized because *the book keeps changing.*"

I resisted the urge to roll my eyes, and covered my chuckle with a little cough.

Every time I think my father had acted as strangely as humanly possible, he'll suddenly do or say something to assure me that there is no shortage of strangeness living within him. He is like an odd well. What's an odd well, you ask? Well, I suppose it's a well that is filled with odd things instead of water. What sort of odd things would be in the odd well, you ask? Well, I don't know. Maybe some glow-in-the-dark pudding, or a two-headed ostrich, or a giant banana that plays the bugle? I don't know. I suppose it's rather odd for me to be devoting so much time toward thinking about what might be in this fictional "odd well," but keep in mind, I am my father's son, which means I'm probably a little odd myself.

Anyway, it appeared as though P was having some sort of mental breakdown. It must have been from the stress of losing all his clients. I tried to be as polite and sympathetic as possible, while also letting him know that he'd gone completely bonkers.

"*Right*," I said to him, nodding my head and patting my father gently on the shoulder. "The *book* keeps *changing*. Of course. Hey, on a completely unrelated topic, maybe you should lie down for a bit? You could probably use the rest. I'm sure that when you wake up, the book won't be *changing* anymore. What do you say, P? Want to rest your weary head? Hmm? It looks pretty darn weary to me."

"Does it?" P asked, feeling the top of his head. "It seems more pointy."

"W. B.!" M cried as she grabbed the book. "Look! He's absolutely right! It's changing!"

She pointed to one of the sentences on the page. When

I took a closer look, I was shocked to find that some of the letters were growing fuzzy and rearranging themselves, marching like ants around the paragraph until they had formed a completely different sentence!

!!!

I rubbed my eyes and then looked again, unable to believe what I'd just witnessed. It was impossible. As a book wolverine, I'd read many, many books in my short life, but I'd never seen one that could edit itself after it'd already been published—not even the ones that could have really used the extra help. I hadn't been looking at the newly formed story for longer than ten seconds before I noticed that another sentence, at the very top of the page, was also changing! And then another sentence, down at the bottom! And then another, on the other side! And the one after it too! Soon, all the letters were turning fuzzier than a lamb's backside, transforming from Ds into Ss, from Os into Hs, from Rs into As, from Cs into Rs, from As into Os, and from Ss into Ns. It was as though the letters in the book had all come to life and decided to tell a whole new story

that they'd written themselves.

"Is this magic?" I gasped, feeling my hands begin to tremble with fear. "What's happening?"

"Don't be silly, W. B.; there's no such thing as magic."

But no sooner had my mother said that, when suddenly there was a flash of light, followed by a very light cracking noise at the other end of the kitchen. My parents and I looked over and saw that a hardboiled egg had been dropped onto the floor.

Aunt Dorcas had disappeared. Like a sneeze in the wind.

SERIOUSLY, NO ONE HAS A MINT?

We looked everywhere for Aunt Dorcas, searching every corner of the Baron Estate including the closets, cupboards, luggage chests, attic, work garage, and the barn. We even got Rose Blackwood to help, and she was in a fouler mood than a two-ton tiger with a toothache.

I tried my best to cheer her up. Sometimes I'm good at that.

"Is there anything you want to talk about, Rose?" I asked while we searched through the dark and dusty attic together. It was spooky up there, so I was glad that I didn't have to search through the dim corners of the rarely-visited Baron attic alone. There were rumors that M and P had hidden all sorts of weird and frightening things up there, terrible things, monstrous things, things that my crazy inventor parents would prefer remained secret from the world. (But then again, I'm the one who started those rumors, and I certainly can't be trusted to tell the truth.)

Rose turned to me sharply, and I winced.

I had noticed that in the short period of time since Buddy had broken their engagement, everything that Rose touched had a terrible habit of becoming ripped, cracked, crushed, or thrown across the room with the force of crashing meteorite. This likely wasn't a coincidence.

"No," she said darkly.

"Are you sure? You seem pretty upset."

Rose ripped the top off an old steamer trunk and hurled it across the attic. As it hit the wall, it exploded in a cloud of dust.

"Why would I be upset?" she asked, forcing herself to smile at me.

It was perhaps the least happy smile I'd ever seen. In fact, it looked more like a silent scream. I noticed that her right eye was twitching, and the little vein that ran up her temple was bulging like a balloon that had been slightly overfilled. All the muscles in her face tightened at the same time, and the effect was as unsettling as watching a snake attempting to eat itself. Rose picked up the old globe that was in the steamer trunk and hurled it across the room. It shattered into a billion little pieces. She "smiled" at me again, making my toes curl.

I cleared my throat and tried my best to say something helpful.

"Well, maybe you're upset because you and Buddy Graham broke your engagement, and now you're all alone again, possibly forever?"

This time, the thing that Rose picked up and hurled across the room was me.

Yes, I had hit a growth spurt and was practically the same height as Rose. But you should never underestimate an angry Blackwood. There's a reason why their name is the most feared name in the country. They're physically strong beyond belief. Legend has it, Rose's great grandfather wrestled bears in his free time. Rose's great grandmother would come out and separate him and the bears when it was time for supper, lifting each of them up with one of her freakishly strong Blackwood hands.

So I flew all the way across the room and out the attic window, landing in a peach tree in my mother's fruit garden, which was actually rather convenient, since I was feeling snackish. As I snacked on the peaches in the tree, Rose stuck her head out the window and looked down at me.

"W. B.!" she cried. "Oh my goodness, I'm so sorry! I meant to move you out of my way, not throw you out the window! I'm afraid I lost my temper, and sometimes when I do that, I don't know my own strength. I promise it'll never happen again. Please forgive me?"

"Of course," I said through a mouthful of peach. "I know you're just upset that your wedding was called off, and now everyone in Pitchfork will be talking about it. You have a right to be upset, Rose. I mean, they're all probably laughing about it, and coming up with terrible and funny nicknames for you. I've thought up a few good ones myself, if you'd like to hear them. If I were you, I would proba-bly—"

I didn't have the chance to tell Rose Blackwood what I'd do if I were in her place because she then flung one of her red boots out the window. It clocked me in the head and knocked me off my branch.

As I landed in the grass, about a half-dozen peaches fell out of the tree and bonked me on the head, one at a time.

Rude, rude, rude . . .

Once I'd finished cleaning the peach juice from my ear, I heard the clatter of complicated clockwork. It was M and P, pulling up to the fence in their mechanical horseless carriage, which sputtered and clicked twice more, before finally falling silent. My parents took off their leather riding caps and safety glasses and wiped the residual desert dust from their cheeks with their handkerchiefs. They had driven through the desert to search for my aunt, venturing all the way into Downtown Pitchfork to see if she was visiting any of her friends or favorite spots.

"No luck in town?" I asked. "No one has seen Aunt . . . Dorcas?"

Hmm. That was odd. For a moment I couldn't seem to remember her name. How can a person suddenly forget their aunt's name? Especially when she has a name like "Dorcas"?

"No," M answered quietly. She cleaned her safety glasses with hands that visibly shook.

"And what's even worse than that," P continued, "is that no one in town seemed to have any idea—"

"Oh, McLaron, please don't say it!" my mother begged.

"Say what?" I asked, finishing off another peach and tossing the pit into the bushes. "Why are you two so upset? Does it have anything to do with Buddy Graham dumping Rose? Is everyone in town already talking about that? What mean nicknames are they calling Rose? Are they saying that she stinks too badly to be named after a flower?

Are they saying she should have been named Onion Patch Blackwood instead?"

A second red boot flew out the window and bonked me on the head.

"Ow."

I suppose I had that one coming.

Without explaining what it was that had upset them, my parents jumped from the horseless carriage and rushed into the house. I followed them as quickly as I could, wiping the peach juice from my hands onto my trousers as I ran. We dashed up the stairs, taking them three at a time, before thundering down the hall and into Aunt . . . (Deena? Dora? Dirkle? Is Dirkle a name? Hmmm . . . wait, I've got it!) Aunt *Dorcas*'s room.

Huh. That's the second time I couldn't remember her name. Why was that suddenly happening to me? I'd never struggled to remember her name before, even when I was trying my hardest to pretend that she didn't exist. Was there something wrong with my mind? And is Dirkle actually a name? It sort of sounds like one, doesn't it? But it also sort of doesn't.

My parents flung open Aunt Dorcas's bedroom door and gasped in shock. I looked into the bedroom and sneezed in the most shocked manner possible.

Her room was completely empty.

Gone were the ruffles and lace and doilies on every surface, and the stuffed animals and throw pillows she'd piled on the bed like a cozy fortress, and the collection of creepy porcelain dolls on the shelf (with realistic looking eyes that seemed to follow and judge you when you went inside). Also gone was the weird, flowery perfume smell, which always clung to my aunt like she'd just been sprayed by the world's fanciest skunk.

Now there was so much dust on the floor and cobwebs in the corners that it looked as though the room had been empty for at least ten or fifteen years, if not longer. The windows were so smudged and filthy that staring through them would have been like trying to see to the bottom of a mud pit. There was also a terrible, stuffy, stale stench in the room, like the breath of a gross animal that lived off a simple diet of other gross animals. In short, it was disgusting.

"I don't understand," I said. "What happened here? Where is all of her stuff?"

"Who's stuff?" Rose asked, as she joined us in the doorway of the empty bedroom.

"You know," I said, turning to Rose in surprise. "The stuff of the person we're looking for. Aunt . . . Aunt . . .

what's-her-name . . ."

"Was it Doreen?" P suggested. "Or Darla? Dirndl? Darkle? Is Darkle even a name? It sounds sort of like a name. But it also sort of *doesn't*. Hmmm . . . Dirkle . . ."

"Dirkle . . ." I repeated, rubbing my chin with my thumb and forefinger.

"Dorcas!" my mother suddenly cried, snapping her fingers. "Her name is Dorcas! For some reason, that name is trying its best to sneak its way out of our brains!" She reached into the front pocket of her work overalls and took out a pen. After rolling up her sleeves, she wrote my aunt's name on her forearm. "Everyone, please take this pen and write her name on your arm! Something is trying to make us forget it!"

We all did as we were told, writing the name "Dorcas" on our forearms in ink. Once I had printed the name in my messy handwriting, I stared at it in bewilderment. I had always hated my name, Waldo, but I had to admit it wasn't as bad as Dorcas. *Dorcas.* Suddenly that name sounded so strange and foreign to me. It didn't sound like a real name at all. *Dorcas.* It was like I had just learned a word in the secret language of the frogs or something.

I tried my best to remember who this Dorcas person was, but the only picture of her I had in my mind was quickly shrinking, fading into darkness, until it looked like little more than an accidental inkblot on a napkin. It was a shadow from the past that seemed less and less real with every passing second. I started wondering if this person had ever really existed, or if my mother was simply playing a trick on all of us. It wasn't like M to play tricks, but it also wasn't like the rest of us to suddenly forget a family member's existence. We've never done that before.

At least . . . I don't *think* we have.

My father's jaw dropped as he continued to slowly turn through the pages of *The Hilarious Mis-Adventures of the Ridiculous Baron Family*.

"An entire chapter of this book just disappeared," he whispered. "All mention of . . . *Dorcas*, is now gone."

The revelation was like a splash of ice water down our trousers. The four of us stood there in shock, staring into the dusty room of a person who was little more than a hollow reflection in our brains, trying desperately to remember anything about them.

Try to remember a short and boring dream you had

about six years ago, on a random Thursday night. That's what it felt like trying to remember anything about Aunt . . . I had to check my forearm again . . . *Dorcas*. It was impossible. We all searched our minds (I noticed that I managed to finish searching long before the others), but we found no trace of her.

"What's happening to us? And what's causing the book to change?" asked Rose as she turned instinctively to my father. "Mr. Baron, you have to have some idea about why our memories and lives are suddenly rewriting themselves. I can't remember—" she glanced at her forearm, "—*Dorcas* at all anymore. But I know that this room hasn't always been empty. What's going on?"

"Yes, McLaron, you must have some idea what's behind all this," my mother pleaded. "What's happened to my sister? She was my sister, right? Not yours?"

My father took a deep and dramatic breath, and then began to cough violently. There was simply too much dust in the empty bedroom for us to take dramatic breaths. P hacked and wheezed as he stomped his feet, disturbing all the poor spiders that were living in the room as my mother and Rose took turns whacking him on the back. We stepped out of the bedroom and headed for my parents' work garage, which was where we usually went to discuss odd things.

"I don't know for certain *what's* behind all of this," P explained, closing the work garage door and then holding up his copy of the Baron book, "but I do know for certain *who* is behind it."

He pointed to the name of the author of *The Hilarious Mis-Adventures of the Ridiculous Baron Family*, which was printed in tiny lettering on the back of the novel. The printing was so small that we probably would have missed it if P hadn't hovered his magnifying glass over it.

"Written by Werbert Turmerberm," I read aloud. "Wait, that's his real name? *Werbert*?"

"It can't be," said Rose. "No one is named *Werbert*."

"Maybe his mother named him when her mouth was full of caramel."

"Werbert Turmerberm . . ." my mother said as she pinched her chin and wrinkled her forehead. "Why does that name sound so familiar to me?"

"I mentioned him to you many years ago, Sharon," my father told her. "Don't you remember? Werbert? Werbert Turmerberm? My *greatest enemy*? From the Pennsylvania College of Dental Surgery? I had promised myself never to speak his name again, but now it appears as though I have no choice. Werbert Turmerberm is the one behind this."

"Why is a dentist your worst enemy?" I asked.

My father set the book on his workbench and stared sadly out the window.

"Because," he said with a heavy sigh as he began the long, strange, and sad tale of Werbert Turmerberm, "I ruined his life."

"Back in the early 1870s, before I met your mother, I left my home in Valdosta, Georgia to attend the Pennsylvania College of Dental Surgery with my best friend, John Henry Holliday. John Henry and I were determined to become the greatest pair of dentists that the world had ever seen. Better than Pierre Fauchard, even!"

"Who the heck is Pierre Fauchard?" I whispered to Rose.

"I have no idea. But if you ask, I'm sure he'll give you a very long and boring explanation," Rose whispered back. I nodded my head and kept quiet.

"As you might have guessed, dental school was very competitive," P continued, smiling as he thought of his old college days. "You can imagine what it must have been like, a bunch of young, hotshot, future dentists. We were a pretty wild group—rowdy young kids with a shared love of teeth. We were all very good students, though. And the top three students in the class were me, John Henry (whom we all called 'Doc'), and Werbert Turmerberm."

"That seriously can't be his name . . ."

My father ignored me as he began rifling through one of the drawers in his workbench.

"Every student in class wanted to be like me and Doc. Doc was a brilliant man, very clever and funny, though he had a bit of a temper, and would often play cards late at night when he should have been studying. But he was an excellent student. I was also an excellent student, but where I really excelled was inventing new and interesting devices for dentists to use. In fact, a lot of my early dental inventions are still being used by dentists today."

He pulled out a metal invention that looked like a mechanical beaver trap with a leather strap fastened to the back. It was coated with a fine layer of dust and cobwebs, and the hinge creaked like it was badly in need of grease.

"This is one of my earliest dental inventions," he said proudly. "My professors all said that it would change the practice of dentistry forever. It didn't, but they still said it would, which was rather nice of them."

"What is it?" Rose asked.

P smiled.

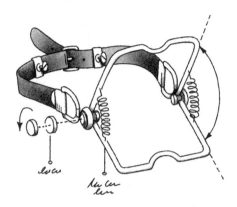

"Why don't I show you? W. B., come over here, please."

"Okay."

I bounced over to the workbench, where P told me to have a seat on one of the little wooden stools. He reached into a drawer and pulled out a cloth cover, which he then wrapped around my neck, as though he was about to give me a haircut. I sat there uncertainly, wondering what might happen next, and then he brought the mysterious invention closer to my face. It smelled pretty terrible.

"Open wide, son."

I looked from the rusty and dusty device, to my father staring at me expectantly, and quickly shook my head.

"No way. That thing is dirty and rusty and gross, P. I don't want it anywhere near my mou—"

Before I could finish my sentence, P had jammed the metal bit into my mouth and wrapped the leather strap around the back of my head, fastening and tightening it to its tightest setting.

I wanted to scream . . . but I couldn't. The device was on some sort of spring, and once the metal part locked into my mouth, it caused my mouth to pop wide open, and stay open. I tried to reach up and undo the straps so I could pull the invention off my head, but I couldn't manage to do that either. In fact, I couldn't move at all! It felt like someone had frozen my arms and legs, and now all I could do was sit there silently with my mouth wide open like a yawning potato.

"This, is my O.W.S. Device, also known as my *Open Wide, Stephen*, Device," P told my mother and Rose. "It's meant for young patients and patients who are afraid of dentists. It keeps them from squirming and shouting and moving around during an examination. In addition to keeping the patient's mouth open, the device also presses against several nerves in their mouth and on the back of their neck that temporarily paralyzes their body. They literally can't move or get away. They can't even scream for help."

"What?" M gasped, looking at me in horror. "You mean you just paralyzed our son?"

"Temporarily," P said, sounding slightly defensive as he undid the strap on the back of my head. "He's fine though. See?"

Suddenly I could move again. I rubbed my aching jaw and smacked my lips. My mouth tasted like I'd just spent the past twenty minutes licking an old shovelhead. There was also a light thudding in the back of my head, as though a common squirrel monkey was gently pounding it with a rubber mallet. That O.W.S. Device was really something.

"Never been better," I choked.

When no one was looking, I quickly stuffed the O.W.S. Device into my back pocket. I wanted to be certain that no one would ever have the chance to put that awful thing on me ever again. Aside from the unnerving feeling of my body being completely frozen, the metal part of the invention also tasted terrible. That dirty and rusty flavor was really lingering in my mouth and was starting to make me feel a bit sick. I wished I had a chocolate cake or a raspberry pie (or preferably both) to cover up the awful taste, and I briefly wondered if P would mind if I took a short break from his story to do some light baking.

"He's fine. Anyway, back to my story. Werbert was jealous of me and Doc because the professors were always praising us for our natural dentistry talents. The other students preferred us to him as well. I hate to say it, but Werbert was a bit of a weirdo."

My mother, Rose, and I, all exchanged a private glance.

My father calling someone a weirdo was sort of like a rotting fish accusing someone else of smelling badly.

"The day before our final exams, Doc and I learned from a friend that Werbert was planning on getting us into trouble with the professors. He was going to secretly place the answers to the final exams in our pockets, and in the middle of the exams, he was going to raise his hand and declare that we were cheating! He was going to try to get us kicked out of school!"

"That swine!" Rose cried.

"What an awful person!" M exclaimed.

"Does anyone have a mint?"

My mouth still tasted like it was filled with wet sawdust and rusty nails. It was pretty foul, and it seemed to be getting fouler by the minute. It was also probably unhealthy for me to have a mouth full of rust, though no one else seemed to be particularly concerned about that.

"When Doc and I learned what Werbert was planning," P continued, "we decided to play a little prank on him instead. While he was asleep in his dormitory bedroom, Doc picked the lock to his room and we both snuck inside. I placed the O.W.S. Device over his head, which paralyzed him. Then we draped his blanket over him, closed his door, and locked it."

Suddenly we all knew what happened next in the story.

"You left the device on Werbert's head so he couldn't take the final exam," M said slowly.

"Which meant he failed his class and couldn't become a dentist," Rose continued.

"Wait, that thing was in Werbert's mouth?" I asked, feeling even more nauseated. "You washed it afterward, right? Right???"

P looked terribly ashamed.

"Not only did Doc and I cause Werbert to fail his final exam, which of course meant he failed out of the Pennsylvania College of Dental Surgery, but after the exam was over, we sort of . . . forgot about him."

"Forgot about him?" M asked, blinking in astonishment. "What do you mean, *you forgot about him*? You forgot that you had placed something on his head that paralyzed him and then locked him in a room by himself?"

"It was a very long and very difficult examination!" P cried, with a deep blush of guilt running across his face. "And afterward, we all went out for a very heavy supper. And you know how tired I get after a heavy supper. It wasn't my fault! It was the supper!"

M and Rose rolled their eyes, but I nodded my head in understanding. If you've ever been seriously distracted and exhausted by food like I have, then you're more sympathetic to others who have been as well. A food coma could be just as debilitating as an O.W.S. Device. One day, I plan to make the medical community aware of people like me and P, who should not be judged by how lazy we become after eating large meals. One day.

"How long did Werbert have to lie there with the O.W.S. Device on his head?" M asked.

P cleared his throat and attempted to smooth down the porcupine spikes of his hair, wincing in pain as they stabbed sharply into the palm of his hand.

"In total?" he asked. "Ummm, well, I'd have to say that he was lying there for about . . . three days."

We all took a deep breath before slowly turning our heads toward the book sitting on the counter: *The Hilarious Mis-Adventures of the Ridiculous Baron Family.*

To be perfectly honest, if someone had done to me what P had done to Werbert, I probably would have written an even nastier book.

"After we graduated from dental school, Doc and I

realized that we had interests other than dentistry. I had much more fun inventing dental tools and devices than I did practicing dentistry, so Doc suggested that I become an inventor. And Doc had much more fun shooting guns, playing cards, and getting into trouble than he did practicing dentistry, so I suggested that he become a politician. Well, it turns out his suggestion was better than mine, because I actually did become an inventor. But shortly after I opened my first inventor's office, I received a special delivery from Werbert."

"I'm guessing it wasn't a letter stating that he forgave you," I said.

P sadly shook his head.

"No. He swore revenge, and told me that since I had ruined his life and his career, he would one day do the same thing to me. Well, it looks like he's done it. My career is ruined. Good old Werbert. It's always good to see someone from the old Pennsylvania College of Dental Surgery succeeding at something."

"That explains the book," I said, "but it doesn't explain what happened to—" I had to read the name written on my forearm, "Dunkas."

"Dorcas," my mother corrected, as she read her own forearm.

I must have smudged the writing on my arm. I was always smudging things up. A regular smudger, I am. I quickly rewrote "DORCAS" and smudged it up almost immediately.

"That's where you're wrong, son," P said solemnly. "Werbert was the sort of fellow who always meant everything he said. Literally. Every word. He never exaggerated, and he never joked. If he ever told you that it's raining cats and dogs out, do not go outside, because you can be certain there are a lot of confused animals falling from the sky. When he wrote that he was going to ruin my life, he meant my *entire* life. Not just my present or my future, but also my *past*."

Rose and I crinkled our brows in confusion, but M seemed to know exactly what P was talking about.

"No, McLaron," M said, quickly shaking her head back and forth. "It's not possible. In fact, it's scientifically impossible. And not only is it impossible, it's also very weird."

After giving my mother a wink and a knowing grin, P quickly shuffled over to the other end of the work garage. Standing in the corner, beside a metal file cabinet containing the blueprints for all of my parents' inventions, was a very tall and wide object covered with a dusty drop cloth. It was P's latest invention, a *top-secret* invention, which was so top secret that not even M knew what it was. M and Rose had all been asking him about it for weeks, but he kept saying that he'd show us when the time was right.

It appeared that the time was finally right.

"You're right about one thing, my little muffin," my father said as he gripped the edge of the drop cloth. "Time travel is indeed quite weird. It is perhaps the weirdest and most confusing concept imaginable, and if you sit around and think about it too much, your mind will likely end up turning into a lump soup. But you're one hundred percent wrong when you call it impossible. Not only is it possible, it has already occurred. Werbert Turmerberm—"

"I still don't believe that's his real name," Rose whispered to me.

"It's like his parents tried to name him 'Herbert' and 'Wilbur' at the same time," I whispered back.

"—has invented a time machine," P declared. "And he is using that time machine to travel back in time to spy on us, so he can write his embarrassing stories about our family in order to humiliate us and ruin our professional reputations. And now that he has destroyed our present and future by turning us into worldwide jokes, he is beginning phase two of his dastardly plan, which is to travel back in time in order to ruin our past. That is what he has done to—" P glanced at his forearm. ". . . Porcas."

"*Dorcas*," M corrected, as she read from her arm again. I glanced at the smudge on my arm and then tried to write "Dorcas" over again, but it just ended up as another smudge.

"Werbert will not stop until he's eliminated each and every one of us from existence, wiping out the Barons forever," P finished, the serious glint in his normally carefree eyes expressing the severity of the situation.

It sounded pretty horrible. In fact, it sounded like it could quite possibly be the worst thing to ever happen to us. I once ate a fried fish sandwich that turned out to be rotten, and I was sick for over three and a half days, but being eliminated from existence sounded even worse than that.

Though that fish sandwich was pretty bad . . . I should have never ordered a second one after I noticed the first one tasted a bit funky. Or a third. And definitely not a fifth. And I really shouldn't have gotten onto that Ferris wheel afterward.

"So, what do we do?" Rose asked.

"How can we fight someone who's in the past?" I asked, rubbing my tongue with my handkerchief in an attempt to wipe away the final foul taste of P's dusty invention. It was really lingering, and it was beginning to make me feel as though I might be sick.

"We must travel to the past as well," P said, a mad grin spreading slowly across his equally mad face. "Werbert has invented a time machine. . ."

He whipped the sheet off his invention with a flourish, like a bull fighter tempting a bull with his red cape. ". . . But I have invented one as well!"

M gasped.

Rose gasped.

I sneezed.

"McLaron!"

"Mr. Baron!"

"Seriously, no one has a mint?"

SOMETHING WENT *BOING*!

My father had certainly invented some strange looking things in the past. He'd built doodads and gizmos and thingamajigs covered in blinking lights, turning gears, electrical currents, steaming pipes, buzzing buzzers, and blooping bleepers. He'd built fully functioning underwater ships, high-powered space rockets, and trousers that looked as though they'd been swiped from a visiting alien. But I don't think any of his older inventions could compare to the strangeness of his time machine.

"It's an outhouse," Rose said, looking very disappointed.

Yes, it looked like an outhouse. A nice and big outhouse, which could probably fit a half dozen people at once (though why you'd want to fit so many people into an outhouse is a gross mystery that I'd prefer not to solve), but an outhouse nonetheless. It was large and wooden and rectangular, slightly splintered and musty, with a half-moon shape carved into the door. There wasn't even a proper door handle on the outhouse; it was just a length of rope that you had to pull to open, like the old and filthy outhouse behind the Pitchfork jailhouse. I don't recommend using that outhouse.

"It's not an outhouse," said P. "It's a time machine."

"It looks like an outhouse," I told him.

"No, it doesn't. It looks like a time machine."

"McLaron, I'm pretty sure that's just an outhouse." M said gently, while patting my father on the shoulder. "Why did you build an outhouse in the work garage? Have you been working too hard lately? Have you been feeling stressed because of those terrible books? That could explain these strange new thoughts about time travel that are floating around your pointy head. I've also noticed you haven't been struck by lightning lately, which might be why your mind is acting a bit funny. Perhaps you should go stand outside in a rainstorm while wearing your hat with the big metal spike at the top. You always feel right as rain after a good lightning storm, even if it does make you smell a bit like BBQ."

P rolled his eyes and exhaled in an exhausted manner.

"You people," he muttered to himself, "sometimes you're absolutely ridiculous."

He pulled the rope and opened the outhouse door.

This time, even I was able to gasp properly.

The moment the splintered door was open we were bathed in a rainbow of bafflingly intense and powerful light. The inside of the time machine was fitted with what looked to be a hundred thousand little lanterns, and yet none of them were larger than a penny. The tiny lanterns blinked and flickered with multicolored life, buzzing and humming and blipping, creating a cloud of static electricity that made my nose tingle and made the hair on top of my head stand up as straight as P's. On the back wall of the time machine was a rectangular glass screen covering a delicate looking panel, which depicted a long line marked with seconds, minutes, hours, days, weeks, months, years, decades, and centuries. Beneath the panel was a series of brass knobs, buttons, and switches meant to control the direction of the time machine. One button was labeled "WHERE" and another was labeled "WHEN".

With its secret grandness exposed, the time machine appeared to be radiating with an unbelievable amount of power and energy. It was like staring directly into the face of a shooting star. I was so awed and impressed that all I could do was stand there and stare, with my jaw dangling loosely from my astonished face as a rainbow of energetic light tickled my cheeks and chin. I didn't have to look at Rose and M to know that they were doing the same thing.

"See?" P said in a satisfied tone. "Time machine."

We all quickly crowded into the glowing time machine as Rose and M began to spit question after question at my father.

"Does this really work?"

"How does it work?"

"Yes, what's powering the time machine?"

"Have you tested it before?"

"Did you go back in time or into the future?"

"Is it safe?"

"Is it dangerous?"

"Is it even a good idea to travel back in time?"

"Yes, what if we accidentally do something that changes the present?"

"Is it possible to alter future events?"

"Couldn't we be responsible for ruining the world if we aren't careful?"

"What are the rules about this?"

"Can we travel back in time to last Thursday when we had that delicious rhubarb pie?"

That last question was actually mine. It might not sound that important to you, but it was a really good pie. It had whipped cream on it.

"One question at a time, please," my father said, holding up his hands to shush us. "Actually, forget that. None at a time. There is no time for questions."

"Sure there is," I said. "We have a time machine. We literally have enough time for everything."

P scratched his chin.

"Good point," he admitted. "Alright. Ask me all of your questions. I'll answer them the best I can. Then, once you're all satisfied, we'll travel back in time to this very moment, and get started right away."

One Hour Later

Sort Of.

I Guess?

No?

Well, We Were Back in the Present after Having Traveled Back in Time for an Hour. So, It Was an Hour Later, Though It Was Actually Still the Same Time as It Was Before We Left.

Does That Make Sense? A Little Bit?

ARE YOU CONFUSED? OKAY, I'M CONFUSED TOO.

LET'S JUST MOVE ON WITH THE STORY, ALRIGHT? ALRIGHT.

"All of your answers make perfect sense. I guess you've thought of everything," M admitted to P. "I suppose it's time for us to get started. W. B., please be careful. You're dripping whipped cream onto the time machine."

"Sorry," I said, finishing the last of my rhubarb pie. "Does anyone mind if we quickly travel back in time again so I can have seconds? And maybe have a glass of milk too?"

"There's no time," P said then scratched his chin again. "Actually, there's plenty of time, but I'm still saying no."

I sighed, but I didn't put up an argument. It was probably for the best. After all, the W. B. from last week looked pretty angry when I showed up and stole his pie. Sucker . . .

"Where are we going first?" Rose asked. "You said that Werbert is currently spying on us and meddling with our past. But that means he could be anywhere."

"He could be anywhere or *anywhen*," M added.

My father lifted a finger to silence us and then quickly flipped through the pages of several of the Baron books, finally stopping when he found what he'd been looking for. He held up his copy of the first book: *The Hilarious Mis-Adventures of the Ridiculous Baron Family.*

"I know where and when he is," said P. "He's currently spying on us during our first major adventure, when we entered the flying Baron Estate into a race around the country. All we need to do is read through this book and pay attention to which lines are changing, and then travel back in time to when those moments actually happened. When the lines in the book are no longer changing, then that means he's traveled elsewhen, and we'll have to read through the other books until we find him."

"Is that really logical?" Rose asked doubtfully. "I mean, why would the pages of the book change just because Werbert is changing events from the past? Wouldn't the book just disappear? Wouldn't Werbert need to rewrite them in order to change them? And why would he do that? None of that makes sense."

"Rose, you're asking for logic while we're standing inside of a steam powered time machine," I told her. "Maybe you should accept the fact that there are some things in life that just aren't going to make sense to you.

That's what I do. Life is easier that way."

M took the book from my father and opened it. After scanning through the first dozen pages, she stopped when her eyes spotted a sentence that was beginning to grow fuzzy. Without looking up, she reached out and adjusted the knobs and dials on the panel of the time machine. That's how clever M is; P hadn't even told her how to set and use the time machine, and she'd already figured out how to do it perfectly. When she had set the time machine to the point in time described by the changing paragraph in the book, my father flipped a switch.

The tremendous Baron time machine flickered and sparked, before disappearing from the present in the blink of an eye.

Traveling through time is very much like falling down a hill (and trust me, I have a lot of experience with both). It's very confusing, slightly nauseating, you can't really see anything very well, often you're screaming, your head hurts, you sometimes lose a shoe, you feel like an idiot for having done it, and you often wonder if you might die at the end.

It makes you feel as though your brain and stomach are trying to trade places with each other, but none of the other parts of your body are willing to move out of the way in order to let them. The feeling is so intense that you begin to wonder if you're suddenly sick with almost every known illness in the world. In fact, as we traveled back in time, I felt as though I had the stomach flu, an earache, chicken pox, pinkeye, tennis elbow, hysterical pregnancy, whooping cough, and an amputated knee, all at that the same time.

Traveling back in time one year was much worse than simply traveling back in time to last Thursday. P explained why as we traveled. He said that traveling through space and time can often . . . something, something, something, blah blah science math bloop math blorp bleep gloop.

Alright. He didn't actually say *blorp bleep* or any of that other nonsense. That's just what my stupid brain heard. I tried to listen to his explanation. I really did. But it was so long and boring and complicated that even Rose and M started yawning and losing interest midway through. I had to ask Rose for a summary of the explanation afterward, and though she couldn't even begin to understand the scientific reasoning behind it, she was able to give me the gist of why we felt so crummy. Basically, the further you travel in time, the greater effect it will have on you. That's why you couldn't do it that often. Travel back in time for five seconds? You'll be fine. But travel back one year? You might need to lie down for a bit. Travel back five years? You probably shouldn't go swimming for a few hours. Travel back one hundred years? You'd better have a bucket handy. And so on . . .

When we finally arrived in January of 1891, I was so discombobulated and confused that I had almost forgotten what we were doing there in the first place.

"I think I need to lie down," I told my family as the door to the time machine opened and I stepped outside, recognizing that we were in my parents' work garage. "Wake me up for supper, please. Actually, wake me in about fifteen minutes for my pre-supper snack. I think I made a pretty good spicy chili back in January, and it should still be in the ice box. Unless of course, me from the future traveled back in time and ate it first. Hmmm . . . I didn't realize that time travel meant I would be competing with myself for meals. I don't think I like that very much. I'm not too fond of sharing with me."

M caught me by the arm and shushed me. I looked at her and raised both of my eyebrows, which is the polite way of yelling at someone when they've just shushed you.

She pointed to the other end of the work garage. I followed her pointer finger and then slapped my hand over my mouth, hoping that I hadn't been heard.

It was M and P from 1891, on the day of the infamous race. M was tied to a table beneath a map of the United States. P was tied to the large steering wheel that was controlling the flying Baron Estate.

An explanation is probably in order.

You see, last year, when my family entered their flying house into an official race around the country, Rose Blackwood snuck into the Baron Estate in Chicago and kidnapped us. She tied up my folks, and she then tried to help us win the contest so that she could use the prize money (and the flying Baron Estate) to break her evil brother Benedict out of jail. I was allowed to go along with her

without being tied up as we traveled around the country, collecting items for the race from various little towns with very strange inhabitants. But the only reason she didn't tie me up like M and P was because Rose didn't see me as a threat; plus she kept a sharp eye on me at all times, and she always kept her little pistol handy. This was before my family knew that Rose was actually a good person who hated to break the law. We didn't realize that she was being bullied by her bank-robber parents and literally forced into a life of crime. We had no clue that she was actually a clever and sensitive person with a keen interest in science. In January of 1891, we were genuinely afraid of Rose Blackwood, and our biggest fear was that she might be just as awful and cruel as her legendary brother.

I looked back at the date and time listed on the glass panel inside of the time machine. It was exactly five minutes after noon. We had traveled back in time to the very beginning of the race. The Baron Estate had just left Chicago, and was headed for its first stop on the East Coast.

"Are we still on track for Stone Lake, Massachusetts, my little muffin?" P from 1891 asked M from 1891.

It was very weird standing there with my parents from the present while watching my parents from one year ago. It was sort of like . . . hmmm, that's not a good comparison. I mean, I guess you could say it was kind of like . . . huh . . . nope, it wasn't like that either. Never mind. Forget it. It's not like anything. I tried to think of something to compare it to, but I couldn't. It was a singularly weird thing that cannot be compared to anything else in the world. If you don't believe me, just wait until it happens to you.

"It looks like we are, McLaron," M from 1891 answered P from 1891. "I see no problems in our future. Well, except for the obvious ones. Do you think that evil woman might harm W. B.? I'm worried that our poor son might be terrified right now, trapped in a room with a murderous bandit. She looked just as dangerous as her evil brother."

Rose from the present looked at my mother from the present with a hurt expression on her face. M from the present shrugged her shoulders.

"I didn't know very much about you back then," M from the present whispered to Rose. "All I knew was that you were the sister of Benedict Blackwood and that you had kidnapped us at gunpoint. If you were in my position, you would have been frightened of you as well."

"It didn't take us long to see the good in you, though," P from the present whispered as well, petting Rose reassuringly on the arm. "Sharon and I are excellent judges of character. If

I'm remembering correctly, I believe we had total faith in you by the time we landed in Massachusetts. Or maybe it was Missouri. It was definitely one of those 'M' states. Or maybe it was Nevada . . . or Idaho? It wasn't Alabama, was it? Hmm. It was definitely one of those states that starts with a letter."

"What was that?" P from 1891 called from the steering wheel, unintentionally interrupting himself. "Sharon, did you just whisper something to me?"

"No," said M from 1891, who was busy using her teeth to guide a giant pointer across the map of the country pasted over her head. She was plotting out the course the flying Baron Estate would take during the race. "You must have heard a noise from the engines or something. Or maybe it was another passing duck."

"Oh?" said P from 1891. "You think that was a duck?"

"Yes," I answered, and then when I saw M and P from the present furiously press their index fingers up to their lips in a gesture that meant *be quiet!* I quickly said, "I mean, quack?"

"You're right," said P from 1891, sounding quite satisfied. "It was just an uncertain duck."

Present M, P, Rose, and I all breathed a silent sigh of relief, as we started to tiptoe across the work garage, edging toward the door leading to the kitchen so we could begin our search of the house.

I know I've mentioned that I'm clumsy. But if you've never heard about my other adventures (the true stories, I mean, not the ones written in those stupid books by Werbert Hermabermamerm-whatever his name is), then I don't think you fully understand how terribly clumsy I can really be.

The last time I was in the flying Baron Estate, I ended up hanging from Aunt Dorcas's bedroom window by my fingertips, not once, but twice, because of my own clumsiness. I also fell down a rocky hill, slipped in a mud pit, was hit in the head by several cans and bottles, and was almost trampled by a pack of wild pigs. And that's only one small fraction of my short lifetime's worth of clumsy misfortunes. You see, I've tripped and fallen so many times that my knees and shins are now a permanent shade of black and blue. I've stubbed my toes so often that they're now all the exact same stubby shape and size. I've been knocked on the head so many times that my skull feels a bit like a wet bag stuffed full of pebbles.

I just have really bad luck. The worst luck. The sort of luck you usually end up with if you cross an evil sorcerer or do something foul to a sacred burial ground or relic. If someone hides a banana peel in a fifty thousand square foot building, I guarantee you that I will slip on that banana peel within two minutes of entering that building. In fact, I'll probably slip on it, fall out of the fifth-floor window, land in a rose bush, and then, when I jump up and scream from the painful thorn pricks, I'll wake an angry guard dog that chases me across the yard, chomping on my backside until I stumble and fall down a well that's gone dry.

That actually happened to me last month. My father had to use one of his inventions to rescue me from the well—an invention he'd invented long ago specifically for the purpose of rescuing me from wells. In fact, he uses that invention so often that the darned thing is starting to wear out.

I'm telling you about how clumsy and klutzy and unco-ordinated I am so you won't be surprised when I tell you what happened next.

As my family from the present tried to sneak out of the work garage without my parents from the past noticing them, I suddenly had a terrible sneezing fit—which is a side effect of time travel that you don't often hear about. As I plugged up my nose with one hand and covered my mouth with the other, the force of my suppressed sneeze shot me backward into the wall of the work garage. The force of my body hitting the wall caused one of the shelves over my head to shake, and the giant metal bell sitting on that shelf rolled off and landed on my head, hitting my skull with a loud CLANG! The CLANG of the bell startled me and temporarily made me lose my sense of hearing. It also made me very confused, so instead of reaching up to take the bell off my head, I panicked, and allowed myself to fall forward like a chopped oak tree. I could hear the frantic skitters of my present parents and Rose rushing toward my falling body so they could catch me before I disturbed M and P from 1891 any further. But just before they could catch me, the heel of my boot got stuck in a knothole in the floor, which spun me around and made me fall in the other direction.

I somersaulted forward and landed inside the large, spare barrel where my father kept his loose nails and screws. The barrel toppled over and landed on its side, with me inside of it, and then, because the flying house was quickly changing directions, the barrel started to roll.

The barrel rolled all the way across the work garage (while I was stabbed repeatedly with a multitude of sharp little nails and screws), until it crashed into the large picture window, creating an explosion of tiny bits of metal, and also causing a large crack to form at the bottom of the glass.

"McLaron!" M from 1891 cried, unable to see because of the way she was tied up. "What was that? Did you hear that awful din? It sounds like the picture window is cracking!"

"A barrel full of nails and screws mysteriously fell over and rolled into the window!" P from 1891 called back to her in his usually cheery tone. "I can't tell you why it happened, my little muffin, but I can tell you it's created a very large crack, and we're going to have to do something about that crack immediately. If we don't, then the pressure of the winds will likely cause the glass to shatter! We'll need to get W. B. or Rose in here to help. Hopefully they can hear us. W. B.!?!?"

I fell out of the barrel with a mouthful (and noseful) of nails and screws. I lifted the ringing bell off my head, spat out a spray of hardware, and turned around, suddenly seeing two sets of parents staring at me intensely.

P and M from 1891 looked at me in surprise, while P and M from the present (who were standing out of sight in the shadows of the far corner of the work garage), held their fingers up to their lips with their eyebrows furrowed, letting me know that I shouldn't tell their past versions the truth about what was happening.

"Yes?" I said to my parents from 1891, shaking the last of the nails from my trousers (and desperately hoping that I got all of them). "What can I do for you, M and P?"

"You can go to my workbench and reach into the top drawer," P from 1891 told me. "That's where you'll find my homemade glass glue. All you need to do is squeeze a little of that glue onto the crack on the window, and in a few hours, it'll be as good as new."

"Which top drawer do you mean?" I asked, trotting over to the work bench, trying to look as unsuspicious as possible. "You have three of them. Did you mean the one on the right, where you keep the *Open Wide, Stephen, Device*, which you once used on your secret sworn enemy, Werbert Terma . . . Terma-meragermummle . . . maberhm? Or something? Him? Or did you mean one of the other two drawers?"

Present M, present P, and present Rose rolled their eyes and buried their faces in their hands. It took me a moment to understand why. It usually takes me a moment to understand things. Sometimes it takes me several moments. I don't understand you people who understand things right away, though maybe I eventually will, several moments from now.

"How did you know about Werbert?" P from 1891 asked suspiciously. "I never told you about my sworn enemy, W. B. Or about my *Open Wide, Stephen*, Device."

"I don't think you've ever told me about your *Open Wide, Stephen*, Device either, McLaron," M from 1891 said to my father, before twisting her upside-down head around so she could get a better look at me. "W. B., why do you look and sound so different? In fact, if I'm not mistaken, you suddenly seem to be at least five or six inches taller than you were the last time I saw you."

"Ummmm," I stalled nervously, looking over at my parents from the present and hoping they could provide me with an excuse. "That's just from the, uh, the altitude! Yeah! The altitude! That's why I seem bigger!"

Altitude. I was proud of myself for coming up with that. I wasn't really sure what it meant, but it sounded like a perfectly reasonable scientific explanation for why I would suddenly look a year older. I looked over at my present family and shot them my winningest grin. They once again buried their faces in their hands and shook their heads, clearly too proud of me to speak.

"The altitude?" M from 1891 repeated with a quizzical frown. "By altitude, you mean our height in relation to the ground below? How would the altitude make you significantly taller and make your voice sound deeper? Also, I've never seen you wear those clothes before. And I've definitely never seen you wear those boots. And I've *certainly* never seen you wear that badge on your vest, which, for some reason, states that you're the world's greatest grandmother! Everything about you is different! What's going on here, W. B.? Are you even our son? You aren't, are you? You're an impostor!!"

Her voice was starting to sound angrier and angrier, and her face had already turned cross in that special way it always did when M realized someone was lying to her. It was a face that I had learned to fear and for good reason. Nothing good ever comes from seeing that cross face, which was why only a fool would try to lie to my mother again after seeing it, like I was about to do.

"Ummm," I ummmed, slowly turning redder than a sunburned fire ant as I fumbled for an excuse for my already fumbled excuse. "Did I say altitude? I meant . . . *not* the altitude. I misspoke. My apologies. Sometimes I forget what words mean and then I say them anyway. But, you see, there's, there's a perfectly good explanation for why I look and sound different. Scientific, even. A perfectly reasonable and scientific explanation for why I'm not an impostor. You see, it's just . . . uh, your memory playing tricks on you!" M's cross look turned crosser, so I changed my explanation again. "I mean, you're going a little crazy, that's all. Wait, I mean, it's because you're upside down, which as we all know, makes people appear taller and older." Her jaw clenched and her eyes narrowed, which frightened me, and made me change my explanation yet again. "Or, actually, the truth is . . . it must be the fumes you've been inhaling while tied up here in the garage. Those fumes are making your eyes see things that aren't really there. You're just hallucinating. I'm actually not here right now. I'm upstairs, taking a bath. That sounds like a scientific explanation, right? Right? Bloop bleep bloop?"

"McLaron," M from 1891 said to P from 1891, "I think we should call for help. There's another stranger onboard the Baron Estate, one who looks a lot like our son, but who is clearly *not*. I don't trust him. He looks dangerous, and he's clearly deranged. He probably spied on our son to learn some of his silly mannerisms and speech patterns, and then snuck onto the Baron Estate back in Chicago. Call for Rose Blackwood. We need to make sure that our real son is still onboard, and that this jittery little crook didn't do something to him."

"No," I begged, "wait, please just let me explain, M from 1891!"

"M from 1891?" P from 1891 repeated with a frown.

"Uh, did I say M from 1891? I meant just regular M. From the present. Where I'm from too. The present. Present W. B. is me. Not from the future or anything. Please just give me another moment to explain, and I—"

"I think we've heard enough of your explanations," M from 1891 interrupted, her eyebrows narrowing beneath her spectacles, and her expression turning colder than I'd ever seen it turn before. I knew from personal experience that one of the only things M hated more than being lied to, was when a phony impersonated her child (it'd happened once before, believe it or not). "And don't call me M. That's what my son calls me. McLaron, call for Rose Blackwood right this second. If you don't, then I will. I doubt Rose will be happy to learn that we have a little stowaway here, so there's a chance she won't even want to land the floating Baron Estate before we get rid of him, if you know what I mean."

"It's actually not floating," I explained to M from 1891. "It's flying. There's a big difference between a floating house and a flying house, right P from 1891? I mean, right, regular P?"

M and Rose from the present exchanged panicked looks, while P from the present began to search through his pockets. He found a pickle, and paused to quietly eat it, before resuming his pocket-search.

"Rose?" M from 1891 yelled, clearly not interested in hearing my explanation. "Miss Blackwood? Please come in here! I think there's something you'd like to see!"

I winced.

Rose Blackwood from 1891 was very different than Rose Blackwood from the present. She wasn't actually evil, or even a criminal, and she certainly didn't mean us any harm. But she wasn't yet acquainted with the strangeness of my family, and she was likely feeling quite nervous (I'm sure everyone is very nervous the first time they kidnap someone), and she was also armed with a little pistol that she regularly threatened us with if we showed signs of disobeying her. How would Rose from 1891 respond to walking into my parents' work garage and seeing two P's, two M's, an older W. B., and another version of herself? Even an exceptionally kind and gentle person might get frightened if they were to see something like that, and then they might do something foolish. I know if it were me, I'd do something ridiculously foolish, if only to prove a point.

"I don't think it's necessary for you to call for Rose Blackwood, my little muffin," P from 1891 said to M from 1891.

"What?" M from 1891 asked in surprise, after shooting

me one more bitter look. "Why not, McLaron?"

"Because of this," said P from 1891, twisting his left wrist until a long, metallic device slipped out of his sleeve. At the end of the metallic device was a little round mirror. It looked like a little dental tool, the kind of long and skinny instrument that a dentist uses to look at the teeth in the back of your mouth. "We can simply ask the people standing behind us. Hello! I knew you were all back there. I could see your reflections in the picture window, and now I can see them all a bit clearer. Ah. Now it all makes perfect sense to me. My little muffin, please allow me to introduce you to me, to you, to W. B., and to Rose Blackwood . . . from the future."

There was no point in hiding it anymore. We'd been found out. My family and Rose from the present stepped forward and waved to P and M from 1891. The past and present Barons eyed each other warily, uncertain how one is supposed to talk to oneself. But eventually, P from 1891 and P from the present broke the ice, and introduced themselves, which I suppose was rather pointless, or at the very least, repetitive.

After everyone had shaken everyone's hands (and after Rose from the present explained to P and M from 1891 that she wasn't really a criminal, and that she actually worked for them in the future), P from the present pulled a strange, new device from his pocket. It was a device that we had never seen before, though we could tell from the delicate way he held it that it was a very important and unique invention, the kind that couldn't be easily fixed or replaced. It looked sort of like someone had crossed a rat trap with a light bulb, and then sprinkled the entire mess with some multicolored confetti.

There was a little panel on the back of the device, and after P opened the panel and flipped a little switch, something went *BOING!*

My Mother Had Always Looked Like a Muffin . . . Hadn't She?

"*Boing?*" I said, turning to P from the present. "What just went *boing*? Was that thing supposed to go *boing*? None of your other inventions have ever gone *boing* before. *Boing* isn't a very reassuring sound. Good things don't usually go *boing*."

"Stop saying *boing*," said M from the present, then she looked over at present P. "McLaron, what was that strange device? What did you just do?"

P from the present was staring wide-eyed at his little device, and smiling as brightly as a human can possibly smile. He looked like a kid who'd just been handed a banana split with extra cherries on top.

"It worked," he whispered gleefully to the device while doing a little happy dance all by himself. "It actually worked. I can't believe it!"

"Congratulations, P," I said. "What worked?"

"Look at Sharon and me!" P declared, pointing behind us.

We looked over to P and M from 1891. 1891 M's head was still crooked toward us, turned at an uncomfortable angle on the table. P from 1891 was still looking at us while strapped to the steering wheel of the flying Baron Estate. But neither of them was moving or making a sound.

In fact, nothing was really moving or making a sound. The coal burning furnace, which typically rumbled like my belly did after I had gone a few hours without eating, was oddly silent as well—which reminded me, I had just gone a few hours without eating.

Actually, no. I had gone even longer! I had traveled back in time one whole year, which meant I'd just gone an entire year without food! A whole year! Without food! Me! My stomach suddenly felt as though it was trying to digest itself because it was so empty. My head felt lighter than a feather. My hands began to tremble. My spine felt so terribly frail. My weakened knees were shriveling up into two little prunes incapable of supporting my body, and I was about to topple forward in a starving heap, when suddenly Rose Blackwood (from the present) caught me by the arm.

"I'm withering away into nothing . . ." I whispered, "please try to go on without me . . ."

"Knock it off, W. B.," she said, giving my bicep a squeeze. "I know you think you haven't eaten in a year, but you're wrong. That's not how time travel works. You just ate that pie fifteen minutes ago, remember?"

"Wrong," I told her. "I ate that pie almost a year from now. In fact, I technically haven't even eaten it yet, since it technically hasn't even been baked yet. And what makes  you an expert on how time travel works? I seem to recall that no one but me believed in time travel until very recently. I was told repeatedly that it was impossible."

"Both of you, please be quiet!" M from the present snapped—I suppose she was getting a little sick of our constant bickering. "McLaron? Please explain what's happened."

"This," P whispered reverently as he held up his new device, which was so unique and awe-inspiring, that it almost appeared to be glowing in the silent work garage, "is quite possibly the greatest invention in the history of inventions. It's possibly the greatest invention that will ever be invented by an inventor. It's an even better invention than the horseless carriage, the Air, Oh! Plane, the submarine, and those mechanical tap dancing shoes that I made last month."

"Oh, those shoes were so annoying," Rose moaned, rolling her eyes at the unpleasant memory.

She was right. Once the mechanical tap shoes started dancing, they didn't stop until you introduced them to a hammer over and over again, beating them into a shiny mess. It took a good six hours of angry smashing before those awful tap shoes finally tapped their final tap. Later that night, my father had buried the tap shoes in the desert, and then, in a rare and confusing show of respect, he played the song "Taps" on his bugle.

M went to the picture window and looked outside. Her eyes widened in shock and disbelief when she spotted a flying V of ducks frozen in midair. Normally, when ducks stopped flapping their wings while hovering high in the sky, they come crashing to the ground. But these ducks seemed to be stuck up in the sky, as if hanging from an invisible thread, and so did the flying Baron Estate. We were all frozen in the silent sky, and there was only one explanation for why.

"You've frozen time," M said to P in an awed whisper. "McLaron, how on earth did you do that? If time travel is impossible, then freezing time is . . . is . . . whatever is beyond impossible. It's impossibler."

"It's impossiblest," I corrected.

"Neither of those are words," Rose muttered.

As my father from the present excitedly explained his crazy and impossiblest invention to M from the present (bleep blop booop blorp), letting her know why all of us from the present weren't frozen as well (gloop blop gleep blarg, and so on) Rose Blackwood and I slowly walked up to P and M from 1891, and stared closely into their still eyes. It was like staring into the face of a statue, only much more familiar and lifelike, and instead of being made of marble or granite, it was made of whatever my parents are made of.

"They're really frozen stiff," Rose said in a hushed voice. "This is so weird. I wonder if they can see and hear us."

I reached out and patted P from 1891 on his frozen spiky head.

"P?" I whispered. "Hello? Are you in there?"

"Stop patting my head, W. B.!" I heard my father say,

and I jumped back and pulled my hand away as though it had been burned. It took me a moment to realize that it was P from the present who had said that, not P from 1891, who was still immobile. Which made more sense.

"Now that we have frozen time," P continued, "we'll need to find Werbert as soon as possible. I'm willing to bet that he's hiding somewhere in this house, trying his best to ruin all of our pasts as well as our futures. Please, everyone, be very careful. He might not look particularly threatening, but Werbert is a very dangerous man. There's no one on earth more dangerous than a failed dentist."

"Wait, won't Werbert be frozen as well?" Rose from the present asked. "How can a person be dangerous if they're frozen?"

And then we all heard something. Normally that wouldn't be a cause for alarm (we heard things all the time), but at that moment, it was particularly upsetting. You see, there shouldn't have been any sounds in the Baron Estate other than the sounds that me, P, M, and Rose from the present were making. The rest of time was frozen, which meant it should have been unable to make a sound.

But we had all heard it. A pair of footsteps, scampering quickly through another part of the Baron Estate.

"No, he's not frozen," P from the present whispered,

a perfectly fascinated smile forming on his face. "He's moving around, just like we are. And I know why. Since he's not from this time period, then that means I can't freeze him here. You can't freeze someone in time if they're already out of time. And do you want to know something else that I find quite interesting? My gut is telling me that Werbert doesn't just have a time machine. He has his own version of a *Time Stopping Device* as well."

"No," M whispered.

"That's impossible," Rose croaked.

"Time Stopping Device?" I said. "That's the name you gave your invention? Not the *Stop the Time Please, Stephen, Device*, or something like that?"

"Of course not," P from the present said stiffly, frowning at the very thought. "That would be a silly name."

P, M, Rose, and I (all from the present) slowly crept out of the work garage and into the kitchen. It was an absolute mess. The cabinets had all opened during the herky-jerky trip across the sky, and most of the plates and cups stacked inside had fallen out and smashed on the floor. There was also the residual mess from when our old horse, Magnus, had become frightened when the house first took flight, and kicked several holes into the oven, wall, and cupboard door. The room looked like a disaster area, but it was otherwise empty.

"Where's 1891 Rose and 1891 W. B.?" M asked.

"If this is the beginning of the race, then that means W. B. and I are in the living room," Rose explained. "But what does it matter where W. B. and I are if we're looking for Werbert?"

P lowered his voice as he led us across the kitchen.

"Werbert has already erased . . . someone, from our minds."

Not only had P forgotten the name of the person we were looking for, he'd also forgotten that we'd all written the name on our forearms. I rolled up my sleeve and looked at what I'd written there in pen. It was just smudge. Huh. Was it possible we were looking for someone named Smudge? I sort of liked that name. Smudge. It sounded a bit like a small serving of fudge—Smudge. Smudge of fudge. Smudge Baron had a nice ring to it too.

"Dorcas," M said as she read the name written on her forearm. "Her name is Dorcas. Oh dear. It appears that the ink is starting to fade again even though I keep tracing over it. Soon we won't be able to read her name at all."

Dorcas! That's right, that was the name! I liked Smudge better, to be honest.

"We have to move cautiously and keep our eyes open at all times," P explained to us as he placed his Time Stopping Device into his pocket. "I don't want anyone else to be erased. Particularly me. I don't think I'd do very well with being erased. Existence is one of my favorite things."

"But how can he erase us if we're already here?" Rose asked. "Let's think about this logically, alright? If he got rid of . . . *Dorcas* during the race, then it wouldn't erase her from our memories. Right? We would just have a new memory of her disappearing during the race. You would still have your memories of her from before the race began. Right? This doesn't explain why it suddenly seems like she never existed in the first place. None of this makes sense."

"She's right, McLaron," said M as she bit her fingernails. "Werbert must have traveled further back in time when he erased . . . Dor . . . Dor . . ." She frowned, unable to read the name printed on her forearm anymore. It kept fading and fading. "Dor . . . whatever-her-name-is. He must have done something to stop her from being born!"

We heard another set of footsteps quickly scurrying through the Baron Estate, followed by a high-pitched snicker which sounded as though it was coming from the walls.

"It's definitely Werbert," P said quietly. "I'd recognize that silly sounding snicker anywhere. And to answer your question, Rose, you're absolutely right. Werbert must have traveled further back in time and done something to prevent D— I can't read my writing anymore either—to prevent whoever-it-was from ever being born. He just came back here to our race around the country in order to toy with us, and perhaps do something else that'll ruin our lives for good. Or maybe he's already done something else at another point in time, and now he's just watching us so he can see us suffer when the change finally occurs. The awful possibilities are endless when it comes to a madman with a time machine. We've already lost one person to time travel . . ."

"Oh dear," said M, turning a sickly color as the last of the pen markings faded from her arm—the last connection to the mystery person disappearing for good. "Poor . . . whoever-it-was."

Poor whoever-it-was indeed. I suddenly felt terrible for this person I couldn't remember. I bet they were nice, and friendly, and generous, the sort of person who would surprise you in the middle of the day with a freshly baked strawberry cake. But even if they weren't, even if they were loud, and boring, and irritable, and fussy, and finicky, and eggy, no one deserves to be erased like an old math equation from a chalkboard. I wouldn't even wish that on my worst enemy.

"But," P interjected, suddenly lowering his voice to just above a whisper, "I've given the matter some more thought, and I don't think that's what Werbert intended to do. I don't think he intended to erase this other person from our lives. I think it was a mistake."

"A mistake?" I asked.

"What do you mean, a mistake?" M asked P. "If he didn't want to erase that other person from existence, then what was Werbert trying to do?"

As he turned to her, P's eyes suddenly looked sadder than I'd ever seen them look before. He reached out and brushed a lock of hair from M's face, then he pulled her in for a hug.

"I think, my little muffin," he whispered, "Werbert was trying to erase *you*."

We found W. B. from 1891 in the corner of the living

room with a vase stuck over his head. He was lying on the floor, looking about as foolish as you'd expect a kid with a vase stuck over his head to look. Rose Blackwood from 1891 was staring at him with a very confused expression on her face, her hand outstretched as though she wasn't sure whether to help him up or to point at him and laugh. They were both frozen stiff, just like M and P from 1891.

"I remember that," Rose from the present said with a giggle. "I couldn't believe how clumsy you were, W. B. In fact, I still sort of can't believe it."

"Werbert isn't down here," P told us after he finished scanning the living room. "Sharon, you and I should check upstairs for him. Rose and W. B., please wait down here. If you happen to see Werbert, yell for help, and we'll come running."

"Wait!" I called as my parents started up the stairs. "How will we know what he looks like?"

"Well," P said thoughtfully, "I haven't seen Werbert in about twenty years. But the last time I saw him, he was short and skinny with frizzy brown hair. He wore little spectacles, and was always dressed in a very drab looking suit with a long tie and ugly suspenders. And if that isn't a good enough description, you'll recognize him by the fact that, unlike everyone else in this flying house from 1891, he'll actually be able to move."

We heard another rustling sound from somewhere in the Baron Estate, and P and M wordlessly dashed upstairs, leaving me and Rose from the present standing there, staring at our frozen past selves. It was amazing how much had changed between us in just one year. Not only did we both look completely different (I was much taller now, and Rose had a much kinder smile), we also both *looked at each other* differently as well. Back then, Rose Blackwood was a nightmare to me—just hearing her name was enough to make my knees knock together in fright. I thought she was a monster. But now she was like a sister to me, and I couldn't imagine my life without her.

"I was so scared of you back then," I said to Rose as I pointed to the frozen versions of us from 1891. "I thought you'd be just as evil as your brother."

"I was pretty frightened too," she replied, mussing up my hair affectionately. "This was the first and only crime I've ever committed. I had more butterflies in my belly than a greedy toad in spring."

"Well, I couldn't tell. You seemed like you knew what you were doing."

"Thanks, W. B." she punched me affectionately on the shoulder.

"What about me?" I asked. "Did I seem like I was handling being kidnapped pretty well? Were you impressed by me too? Did you think I was very brave?"

Rose raised an eyebrow as her lips curled up into a smirk.

"W. B., look at yourself."

I looked over at W. B. from 1891. Not only was there a vase stuck over his head, his pants had also split. And there was a mustard stain on the back of his shirt as well. How the heck does a person get a mustard stain on the *back* of their shirt?

"So what?" I said indignantly. "You can be clumsy and brave at the same time."

Rose laughed.

"W. B., I've seen you do some incredibly brave things. In fact, you're probably the bravest kid I've ever known. But on the first day I met you, you seemed so jittery and nervous and clumsy and frightened, that I just felt really sorry for you. Every time I showed you my gun, you looked like you were about to faint or throw up or both. One of the reasons I started hiding the gun in my handbag was because of how pathetically frightened you looked whenever you saw it. I felt pity for you."

Before I could tell her that W. B. from 1891 didn't

need her pity, we both heard a very unsettling sound. It was another high-pitched giggle, followed by the pitter patter of furtive footsteps scampering across the first floor of the Baron Estate. In fact, if my ears weren't deceiving me, it sounded as though the person creating the footsteps was making their way down the hall at that very moment and was about to dash into the living room! Rose and I both spun around with our fists held up like boxers, hoping to catch and pummel my father's mortal enemy the moment he crossed the doorway.

But he never appeared. We stood there for another thirty seconds, crouched in wait, fisticuffs ready, while trying to hide the fact that we were both shaking like a bowl of watery jelly in the middle of an earthquake. I looked at Rose Blackwood's trembling fists and hid a smile—it was good to know that I wasn't the only one who was afraid. She saw me staring at her shaking hands, and her cheeks turned bright red.

"W. B., I refuse to stand here and shiver like a frightened kitten," she told me as she stood up straight, quickly hiding her shaking mitts in her pockets. "We know Werbert is here somewhere. Your parents had us split up so we could look for him upstairs and downstairs simultaneously, and I think that was a great idea. Now I think that you and

I should split up too, so we can properly search the downstairs of the Baron Estate. We need to make sure that Werbert can't sneak from room to room as we search for him, hiding in places that we've already searched. I'm pretty certain that that's what he's been doing to stay hidden from us. Please be as brave as I know you can be, W. B., because our existence is at stake here. The moment you see Werbert, scream as loud as you can, and your parents and I will come running. Alright?"

"Alright, good plan," I said, "I'll go check the kitchen."

Rose caught my arm as I started to leave the living room, my mind already considering the country ham that I knew we still had in the larder in January of 1891.

"I think it might be a better idea if *I* check the kitchen. Otherwise, you might get distracted, and then forget to check the other rooms too. Why don't you search your parents' bedroom and my bedroom, and I'll explore the kitchen, garage, and all of the downstairs closets. We'll meet back here in ten minutes. Good luck, kid."

As Rose carefully stepped through the swinging door into the kitchen, I slowly made my way down the hall to my parents' bedroom. My frightened legs twitched with every uncertain step I took. My heart was pounding so loudly in my chest that it was beginning to give me a headache. I was suddenly feeling more frightened than I'd ever felt before, which unfortunately meant I'd have to be braver than I'd ever been before. There were few things in life I hated more than having to be brave, but unfortunately, I rarely had much of a choice in the matter. I would have to be brave, if only to prove a point to Rose. She had told me that she thought I was a frightened and clumsy mess when she first met me. And while that might be partially true, I certainly didn't want to prove her right, especially not when my entire family's existence depended on it.

When I threw open the bedroom door, I was blinded by a terrific flash of brightness, as though a bolt of lightning had struck in the middle of the room, creating an explosion of sparks.[1] I didn't know what to do, so I dropped to the ground and covered my head with my hands, hoping that my father's time-freezing invention hadn't accidentally done something silly like destroying the entire universe as we know it. When the bright light finally cleared, and I lifted my head up from the ground, I saw that there was

---

1. That actually happened in M and P's bedroom once before. Two years ago, P had been struck by lightning while he was sleeping in bed. But by that point, he was so used to being struck by lightning that he didn't even notice. He just mumbled to my mother something about turning off her lantern when she was finished reading, rolled over, and fell back asleep. If the tip of his sleeping cap hadn't caught fire, he probably wouldn't have believed that it actually happened.

no one in my parents' bedroom. It was just as it always was, but it was also . . .

. . . different?

It was definitely different, though I couldn't say precisely *why* or *how* it was different. Something was wrong though, I could smell it like a cookie baking a mile away. Something had been changed, but it wasn't a major thing, not like the significant change that had occurred in the empty room upstairs which had belonged to . . . whoever it was that it had belonged to. This was a small change, tiny enough to not seem crazy, but large enough to be noticeable, and to eventually drive me a little bit crazy.

As I stood there and stared at the familiar and yet noticeably different bedroom, I heard a terrified scream, followed by another wild giggle. The giggle echoed throughout the entire Baron Estate, and then it slowly began to fade, as though the giggler had opened the back door and jumped out while still giggling.

I rushed out of the bedroom just in time to see the entire living room light up as though there'd been another explosion. I once again dropped to the ground, covering my head with my hands, though this time I mistakenly forgot to protect my face as I dropped, resulting in me getting a rather painful and unpleasant rug burn across my forehead, nose, and chin.

"Rose?" I called blindly into the dusty floor (while wishing that I had actually swept the floor on that day in 1891 like I was supposed to, instead of just lying to M about it). "Rose, are you alright?"

"W. B.?" Rose cried as she stumbled into the living room from the kitchen, looking baffled and dazed. "What was that sound? The lights flashed twice and then I felt something rumble throughout the Baron Estate. I thought that someone might have lit a stick of dynamite or something. What happened? Did you see?"

"I saw the lights flash and heard the rumbling, too, but I don't know what actually happened. On a completely unrelated note, does my parents' room look strange to you now? Am I crazy, or is something different in here?"

Before Rose Blackwood could answer, I saw P thunder down the stairs, followed by my slowly moving mother (who preferred not to thunder if she could avoid it). The moment I spotted them, my eyes did a double-take, as though they couldn't believe what they'd just seen.

But I couldn't tell you why they had done that.

In fact, a few seconds later I felt quite embarrassed for doing the double-take in the first place. It was just my parents. My father and my mother, the same father and mother I'd known for my entire life. My eyes should have done a single-take (which I guess is called just regular old looking), though for some reason, they didn't. Curious. My mind was beginning to fill up on curiosities, mysteries, and confusions, and it had no idea what to do about them all.

"Did you see him?" P asked us. "Did you see Werbert?"

"McLaron, take me back to the present right now!" my mother ordered P before Rose and I could answer. "My feet are swollen and my head hurts. And I haven't had a decent cup of tea in almost one hour! You know I need my tea! It helps my digestion! And my allergies! And my knee pain! And my temper! And my uncontrollable shouting!"

"I'm sorry, my little muffin," P said to my mother with a sympathetic grin. "But it's very important that we find Werbert as quickly as possible. Otherwise, he'll grow tired of toying with our lives, and then he'll erase us all from existence. I have to say that the most terrifying part about all of this is that we have no idea how much he's already interfered with our lives. He could have already changed something huge, erasing a key person or event from our minds, and we would never even know about it. We'd naturally forget all about how our lives used to be. He could change everything we believe forever."

"That's nonsense!" my mother snapped as she adjusted

her hair. "Everything you say is nonsense, codswallop, poppycock, and podsnappery! And stop calling me *your little muffin*. Do I look like a muffin to you? Do I? Huh? Hmmm?"

Rose and I exchanged a secret look. She *did* sort of look like a muffin. Her shape was undoubtedly muffin-ish, her hair looked like a muffin-top, she smelled a bit like a pan of stale muffins, and the blue beads she wore on her dress looked exactly like the blueberries on a blueberry muffin. All and all, she probably couldn't have looked more like a muffin if she was sitting on a plate beside a giant mug of coffee.

"I'm sorry, Madge," P said to my mother. "I forgot how much you hate that. I'll take you back to the present right away, and then we'll continue our search in the past while you rest and drink your tea."

"Hurry up!" she snapped. "I need a hot bath immediately, or I might start to become a bit unpleasant."

My mother had always looked like a muffin . . . hadn't she?

I REALLY HATE NOT EXISTING

After my father dropped off my thoroughly annoyed mother back in the present, he, Rose, and I began to flip through all of the Baron books in search of fuzzy moving letters, so that we could see where Werbert had gone next. P had been clever enough to bring several copies of the Baron books with him, which meant all three of us could constantly be flipping through them to check for changes. We figured that three sets of eyes would give us a better chance of spotting a change just as it was occurring—it was of the utmost importance that we catch Werbert before he could finish altering or erasing any more of our history. Since we were clearly running out of time, we would have to be very quick and very smart to stay one step ahead—er, behind?—Werbert.

"Ouch," I cried, having given myself a paper cut for the fourth page in a row while flipping through my copy of *The Idiotic Imbecilities of the Ridiculous Baron Family*. Coincidentally, the W. B. on the cover of that book had just given himself a paper cut as well, though I must say I was weeping in a much more brave and tough manner than he was—there was barely even any mucus running out of my nose as I cried.

We were searching intently for a good five or ten minutes, our eyes scanning every inch of the pages, before Rose finally spotted a slowly changing sentence in her copy of *The Underwater Bungles of the Ridiculous Baron Family*.

"He's in the submarine!" Rose cried. "He traveled back in time to when we were taking the long submarine ride to that island in the middle of the Pacific Ocean! We need to get there right away!"

"To the time machine!" P declared.

"Oh no," I muttered quietly.

The submarine adventure. Of all the places for Werbert to go . . .

I must admit that I've enjoyed most of my family's adventures, even the really intense and frightening ones that almost cost me my life, which, come to think of it, has been most of them. But I didn't enjoy the time that we spent in the submarine my father invented. In fact, it was one of the most miserable experiences of my life. It was cramped in that cursed submarine, it was boring, we eventually ran out of food, the view was very repetitive, and there was a smelly monkey living in there who made it his life's mission to make certain that I was as unhappy and uncomfortable during that submarine trip as humanly possible. In the end, that monkey had actually saved my life, but that didn't change the fact that he spent over six weeks torturing me in an enclosed underwater ship. Lousy, stupid, lifesaving monkey . . .

P, Rose, and I felt the time machine land with an oddly metallic sounding clang, which rang throughout the invention like a struck gong. But even from inside the time machine, I could still smell the strong ocean air outside, which presumably meant we'd reached our destination. I suddenly wished for a window in the time machine; we had no idea where exactly we'd landed.

"Where are we?" I asked.

"Why, we're in the submarine, of course," P said proudly.

"You managed to land the time machine directly inside the submarine?" Rose asked P. "That seems unlikely. You'd be hitting a moving target while traveling in a vehicle that passes through space and time. You'd need to be pretty darn precise with the control panel in order to do that."

"I suppose that's true," P answered with a grin and a wink, "but as we both know, Rose, I'm nothing if not precise. Precision is my middle name."

He opened the door to the time machine, took a step forward, and immediately dropped out of sight. Rose and I rushed to the edge of the doorway and looked down, breathing a sigh of relief as we saw P crumpled on a floating bed of metal, moaning in pain, but otherwise safe and sound.

In case you were wondering, P's real middle name is Aaron.

The time machine had landed on top of the submarine just as it had surfaced in the middle of the Pacific Ocean; I suddenly remembered that we had done that several times during the submarine adventure, surfacing for the opportunity to get some fresh air and to gaze at the beautiful surface of the sea. It was especially pretty in the early morning and afternoon, when the bright rays from the sun skipped across the frothing white capped waves. Those occasional breaths of fresh air were one of the only things that kept us sane during the long and tedious journey across the sea. They were our reminder that there was a world outside of that cramped little tin can that we were all stuck in, which smelled much too strongly of monkey for my liking.

Rose and I jumped out of the open time machine door and landed on the familiar metallic top of the submarine. It was slick from being underwater, but miraculously, neither of us slipped and fell.[2] As I helped P to his feet, Rose pounded on the circular door at the top of the submarine and screamed for someone to open up.

"I wouldn't bother knocking on the door, Rose," P told her. "We can't hear you in there. The shell of the submarine is practically soundproof. I designed it that way on purpose so we would have a quick and quiet ride without being bothered by chatty dolphins, singing whales, or belching sharks. You would need to pound on that door with a sledgehammer in order to be heard."

---

2. I'm often the butt of the joke when it comes to my inexplicable and unbelievable acts of clumsiness, so I'd like to take this opportunity to point out once again that I DID NOT FALL HERE. That's right. I am not always a giant klutz, believe it or not. Yes, I might have stubbed my toe a bit when Rose and I landed on the submarine, and I might have also bit my lip, fractured my thumbnail, twisted my ankle, got a slight nosebleed, and dropped my wallet into the sea . . . but I did not fall.

I screamed. Rose screamed. P screamed. And though I couldn't say for certain, I'm pretty certain I heard myself scream from inside the submarine as well. Moments later, we heard the sound of a furnace roaring, bubbles bubbling, and then the steam powered submarine began to slowly sink back into the sea. P, Rose, and I had to quickly climb into the time machine and shut the door, firing it up and forcing it to hover in the air before we were dragged underwater as well.

"Great idea, W. B.," Rose grumbled sarcastically as she tried to close the door to the time machine with one hand while flipping through a Baron book with her other hand. "Now we'll have to catch up with Werbert somewhere else. According to my book, it looks like he's already left the submarine, and who knows what damage he'll have done there—Mr. Baron, would you please help me? I can't seem to get the door closed. It's jammed. Something must have happened to it when we landed on the submarine."

"I've found him!" P cried—he'd been flipping through his copies of the Baron books as well. "He left the submarine in a hurry—I imagine little Waldo must have frightened him away, heh heh, that naughty little monkey. Now it looks as though Werbert's back in the Pitchfork Desert, and according to this book, it's around the time when W. B.'s friend B.W. used my Doppelgänger Device to transform himself into our son. Alright, everyone, we have our next destination!"

"Oh, no," I moaned, plopping down on the time machine floor in exhaustion. "We have to go back and see B.W.? I hated B.W."

"Mr. Baron?" Rose called again. "You never answered me about the door. It still won't shut. Will that be a problem?"

"You hated B.W.?" asked P, his nose twitching in disbelief. "Since when? I remember you two being the best of friends, thick as thieves, two peas in the same pod, a pair of pumpkins from the same patch, two partridges in the same pear tree, a couple of bananas in a hammock. In fact, I was wondering just the other day why I haven't seen that kid around lately. I've missed him."

Another explanation is in order. Sorry for all of these explanations, but traveling back in time has made most of them necessary—well, I suppose they're only necessary if you want to know what's going on. If you don't care about what's going on, then go ahead and skip the explanations. I swear I won't mind. The story will probably be more entertaining that way, or at the very least, it'll be shorter.

You see, B.W. is a kid who I first met in school. At first, I thought we were best friends, but it turned out he was only pretending to be my friend so he could steal my parents' inventions and give them to his father. B.W.'s father also happened to be Benedict Blackwood, who is the worst human being in the history of human beings, in addition to being Rose's brother. After B.W. knocked me unconscious and placed me on an eastbound train, he used a device that my father invented, the Doppelgänger Device, to transform himself into me, so he could pose as W. B. without either of my parents realizing that I was gone. The Doppelgänger Device is a baffling invention that can transform you into someone else with the press of a button—but I couldn't even begin to tell you how it works or why. It might have something to do with altitude. I really don't know.

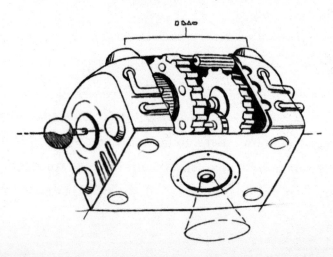

In the end, I'd foiled B.W.'s evil plot, and tied him up before placing him on an eastbound train with a pair of tone-deaf hobos to serenade him for the entirety of the trip. It was a rather cruel revenge that I'd inflicted upon him (the hobos were literally the worst singers on the planet—they sounded like a pair of tortured cats, only not quite as melodic), but sometimes, bad people needed to be punished for doing bad things. Not to mention the fact that B.W. would be less likely to harm me if he were located all the way across the country.

Anyway, those are all the reasons why B.W. hasn't been around lately (people who threaten to one day destroy you as they're carted away on a high-speed train don't often stop by for tea), but there wasn't enough time to explain all of that to P, and he likely wouldn't have listened to the entire explanation anyway.

"Erm, I'll be sure to invite him over for supper next Sunday," I said. "Let's go, P. Before Werbert strikes again."

"Right," said P, and he quickly went to the control panel mounted on the back wall of the time machine, in order to set the time, date, and location to match the changing pages in his Baron book. "Hang on, everyone. To the not-so-distant future!"

"But, the door—" Rose began, but it was too late.

P had already set the brass knobs and the iron levers, and pressed the final copper button and glass switch. There was another flash of light, and a rumbling buzz that reverberated throughout the entire room like a really bubbly burp. The invention released its surge of energy in a suffocating puff of steam, and while the blinking rooftop of the machine began to crackle and spark, every organ in my body did a 360-degree spin as the tremendous Baron time machine took off.

Traveling through time is uncomfortable enough in a confined time machine, but traveling through time in a time machine with a door that was dangling open was about two hundred and fifty-eight times worse. We felt as though we were rattled and flipped by every tiny bump or twist or spin that the time machine experienced during the journey. We kept seeing the literal winds of time whip past us at blinding speeds, brightly colored streaks of history smearing across our sightline like wet paint as the force of our travel pinned us to the ground. Every inch of my skin felt like it was prickling with static electricity. My nostrils and eyes tingled and itched, and my teeth felt as though they were rattling around in my mouth like loose marbles in someone's pocket. I thought I'd felt terribly sick during our maiden voyage of the time machine, but it was nothing compared to traveling with an open door. Occasionally the dangling door would be hit with a gust of wind and slam against the empty frame, splintering and cracking the door jam, and hurting our ears from the sheer volume.

"Shut the door!" P shouted. "Were you raised in a time traveling barn? Rose, it's not safe to travel through time with an open door!"

"I tried! I told you! It won't shut!"

"Why didn't you tell me about that earlier?"

"I did! I told you three times!"

"No, you didn't! I would have remembered that! I always remember things that are told to me thrice!"

"Mr. Baron, with all due respect, you have the memory of a tired goldfish!"

"What? A tired goldfish? If I could remember what we were just arguing about, I imagine that I'd probably be quite offended by that remark!"

As P and Rose continued to quibble, shouting over the uniquely loud and confusing sounds of time travel, I did my best to keep a lookout for Werbert. Even though I was pinned to the floor, I found that if I closed one eye and squinted the other, while looking down and out of the time machine doorway, I could sort of see the places and events in time that we were passing. I couldn't see them with any great clarity, but I could see them well enough to recognize some of them, particularly the events that I had been a part of. I managed to watch the rest of our adventure that had begun in the submarine and ended in the desert, when we defeated a notable conman who had claimed to be the Vice President of the United States. He and his accomplices had eventually been crushed by a creature that had been enlarged by one of my father's brilliant inventions, dragging them all the way down to the far ends of the earth.

It was a pretty great moment in the history of the Barons, a moment where my family had come together to successfully defeat an evil conman, and then return a chest full of stolen pirate treasure to its rightful owners across the world. If I were keeping score, I would have to say that it was one of the adventures that I was proudest of. A smile spread across my face as I stared down at the scene dreamily, watching with great interest while it was replayed on the ground below me—

—though even as I stared down at the scene, watching my family as we decided to fly to Europe in order to return the pirate treasure to its rightful owners, something appeared to be slightly wrong. Much like my parents' bedroom back at the flying Baron Estate, something was a bit "off," a bit "weird," a bit "unexpected and incorrect"—it was sort of like taking a bite of a chocolate chip cookie, and finding that had been baked with salt instead of sugar. If that makes any sense.

The time machine moved a bit further down our timeline, and I then watched my family as we traveled the globe, returning the pirate treasure to its rightful owners in wonderful and beautiful countries like England, Spain, Sweden, and Belgium. We flew across the continent in our unique flying machine—which P had named an Air, Oh! Plane, stopping in several other places in order to takes photographs or pick up unique souvenirs. My memories of the European trip came flooding back as I watched them a

second time, though I must say that I was very confused as I watched my furious and muffiny mother shout and squawk the entire time about how foolish it was for us to not keep the treasure for ourselves. She insisted to every king, queen, and nobleman we met that the treasure was actually owed to us, as proper payment for all of our troubles, and that they were essentially stealing it from us by not offering it back as a reward—which made no sense. It was very embarrassing for everyone. P, Rose, and I were forced to make regular excuses for her, apologizing to the royals who spoke our language and offering blushing shrugs to the ones that did not.

The time machine accelerated, and we left that moment in space and time to move on to whenever it was that Werbert was hiding. But my mind still couldn't shake the obnoxiously persistent thought that what I'd just seen in our timeline was wrong, utterly wrong, preposterously wrong. I wasn't the fastest bat in the cave, but I knew when something wasn't right with my family. P had mentioned that Werbert possessed the ability to change things in our life without us knowing about it, but at that moment I *knew* that he had done something to my mother. Don't ask me how I knew it—I just did. Maybe it's because my brain was a bit different than everyone else's, maybe it was a bit too bruised or a bit too lumpy or a bit . . . I don't know, too squishy, from all my accidents? Anyway, I didn't know what it was, but there was something about my mother that wasn't right, and that made me madder than I'd ever felt before. How dare this lunatic do something to my mother, and why, just because of something stupid that had happened with my father in college over twenty years earlier? That was no excuse. We've all accidentally done things to others that we later regretted. That was just a part of life. People accidentally hurt and upset other people all the time. That is what people do. If you don't like it, then I suggest you try being something other than a person, like perhaps a chameleon (I've heard they're remarkably warm-hearted for cold-blooded creatures). It was certainly not an acceptable reason for erasing other people from existence and transforming perfectly innocent mothers into mean, miserable, misanthropic, maleficent, malicious, miserly, mingy, and muffiny monsters.

As I continued to glower, the anger bubbling and brewing in my belly, I happened to spot something interesting that suddenly appeared directly outside of the open time machine doorway. Floating along the smeared and confusing lines of time, was a tiny little man with a wispy frizz of brown hair. He had tiny spectacles pinched onto the very end of his nose, and he wore what looked to be the single most uncomfortable suit that I'd ever seen a human being wear—it was simultaneously too tight and too loose, and the material bore an uncanny resemblance to the material they use to make onion sacks. It had roughly two hundred and sixteen tiny little buttons on it, all of which had to be fastened for the suit to stay on. I would honestly rather go around in my long underwear than be forced to wear such an awful piece of clothing.

Perhaps the most curious thing about the man was that he appeared to be hovering in midair, flying through time at roughly the same speed as the Baron time machine. His legs were crossed, and he was crouched over a little notebook in his lap, which he was writing in with a very unusual looking pen. I am not exaggerating when I tell you that the pen was an absolute marvel. It looked a bit like a shotgun shell; long and thin, it was made of copper and wood, with little wires and blinking lights running down the sides, and a steady stream of steam billowed from the top as he wrote. The stream of steam also formed what appeared to be a sort of shield around him, which protected him from the quickly whipping winds of time. It was clearly no ordinary pen (if my description still hadn't already made that clear to you), and it took me only a few moments to realize that the floating man was Werbert, and that *the pen was his time machine*. That was how he had been doing it, traveling through time and making dramatic changes, writing terrible books about the Barons while literally rewriting all of our lives. With a time traveling pen.

It was absolutely brilliant: a time machine tiny enough to fit in the palm of your hand! That had to have been the greatest invention I'd ever seen, and I'd seen some pretty marvelous inventions in my time. I realized then how dangerous a villain Werbert really was. My family had faced many different villains during our adventures, but never one as clever as P's mortal enemy. Werbert had invented something that had surpassed P's inventing talents by a great margin, which meant that the Barons were truly at a disadvantage for the very first time since I could remember. Without the power of science on our side, could we defeat this luna-

tic? Could Werbert ever be stopped? What could we do?

"P!" I called, pointing to Werbert as the skinny man began to pick up speed and flew farther ahead. "It's Werbert! I just saw him! He's flying up ahead! His time machine is a pen! And I think I know how he's been ruining our lives! He's literally rewriting them! It's an absolutely brilliant invention, and I don't know if we can stop it!"

"What's that?" P called back to me, pointing to his ear. "It's very loud, but I thought I heard you say something about a brilliant invention, so I'm assuming you just complimented me! Thank you! Yes, I am quite brilliant! You'll have to tell me why you were complimenting me later, though! Everyone, grab ahold of something!"

"Why?" I screamed.

And then I learned why a split second later. The time machine came to an immediate stop midair, and when it did, I was suddenly hurled across the enclosed space, missing Rose and P, but crashing into the edge of the doorway, face first. One of the hinges squeaked as the door shook and rattled, and then the entire thing began to fall from the time machine.

"Catch that door!" my father cried.

Rose lunged forward and caught the door moments

before it dropped to the ground far below, grunting in pain as her ribs scraped the edge of the doorway.

"I'll help you with that, Rose," I said. I crawled forward on my belly while peering over the edge at the familiar Pitchfork Desert below.

I recognized the scene below right away, as it was still quite clear in my memory. It was shortly after the last Pitchfork Fair, when Benedict Blackwood had posed as Rose Blackwood and entered an exploding pie into the fair's baking contest. Rose was then arrested for the crime, and she temporarily moved out of the Baron Estate, which depressed my whole family. As I looked down from the floating time machine, I saw myself walking despondently through the desert, and I remembered feeling so sad, alone, and abandoned, thinking I would never see my good friend Rose ever again. Then I looked a little farther down the desert road, and saw something else, something that I hadn't noticed several months earlier when I had been the one down there doing the despondent walking. It was B.W., crouched behind a cactus, waiting for me to pass by so he could jump out and strike me. He had a lead pipe in his hand, which must have been what he'd used to knock me over the head—afterward, he threw my unconscious body onto a high-speed train in order to get rid of me.

It's pretty hard to sneak up on someone in the desert, so I suppose it was really foolish of me not to see B.W. coming. But I still found myself growing rather annoyed as I watched that little liar slowly creep up on me. I thought about calling down and warning myself about B.W., but I quickly thought better of it. I didn't want to cause any trouble in the past if I could avoid it. I remembered Rose saying something about how changing the smallest things in the past can sometimes have a major effect on the future—a single crushed butterfly or shattered acorn or spilled cup of juice could be the start of something disastrous that would transform the future into an unrecognizable nightmare. That sounded pretty frightening to me, just the sort of thing I'd want to avoid. I didn't want to warn myself about B.W. in the past and accidentally start an unexpected chain of events that would end up with me becoming my own grandfather or something. That's a headache that I absolutely didn't need.

I reached forward in order to help Rose grip the door, but as I did, something inexplicably strange happened; the lights within the time machine flashed, just like they had back at the flying Baron Estate, and then I heard a cracking noise that made me think of a terrible storm. As I shielded my eyes and leaned down farther to get a better grip on the door, Rose Blackwood suddenly disappeared. I mean she literally disappeared. One minute, she was lying there, holding onto the door to the time machine while gritting her teeth and cursing under her breath, and the next minute, she was gone. She had completely vanished, and without her help, the door to the time machine was suddenly falling to the ground at a tremendous speed. I looked down in time to see the door land on my head, knocking me from the past unconscious just moments before B.W. was able to. B.W. stared at the unconscious me from the past, before looking up at the floating time machine, and then staring at me in confusion. I shrugged down at him. He shrugged up at me. I shrugged again and so did he. P was right. It was rather nice to see B.W. again.

I turned back to my father.

"P, what happened? Did you see that? Rose Blackwood just disappeared into thin air!"

P gasped, bringing both of his hands to his mouth as he stared at the spot on the time machine floor where Rose had been not fifteen seconds earlier . . . but then a look of confusion fell over his eyes like a heavy veil. He blinked twice and stared at me strangely, as though I had just asked him to answer an impossible and nonsensical question. I then felt an invisible veil fall over my own eyes as well, and I suddenly knew what he was about to say to me even before he actually said it.

"Who's Rose Blackwood?"

I tried to explain to my father who Rose was, but truthfully, I was already starting to forget. In my mind, I saw the slowly fading picture of a pretty and clever lady with a black hat and red boots, who had saved my life once, and then . . . and then . . . and then . . . and then what? What was it that I was trying to remember again? Something about a hat? My mind suddenly felt so tired and spinny from all the time travel, that I had the overwhelming urge to take a sixteen-hour nap.

"W. B.," my father said slowly. "Who is Rose Blackwood? Why did you say that name?"

Huh? Had I just said the name Rose Blackwood? I didn't remember that. Did I know someone by that name? Maybe it was the name of an old family friend, or someone from school, or maybe it was just a friend of a friend of a friend? It did sound vaguely familiar though, like a name I might have heard in passing. Or maybe my mind was just playing tricks on me. I'd certainly taken a lot of hits to the head throughout my short and rather unfortunate life. In fact, I had literally just watched myself get bashed in the head by a heavy wooden door that fell from about three hundred feet in the air. That seemed like the sort of thing that might leave some long-lasting damage to the old noggin, doesn't it? Maybe my mixed-up mind was just imagining people and names—Rose Blackwood. Huh. Interesting name. It sounded slightly evil. Maybe it was a character from a book that I'd read long ago, or maybe it was from a dream I'd once had. But I supposed it was nothing that I should waste too much time thinking about, not when we were busy chasing a mad villain through space and time, with only a terrible series of poorly written books to serve as our guide.

"I don't know, P," I admitted. "Sorry, I thought I knew someone by that name, but I guess I was wrong. Should we continue to check the Baron books to see if we can find exactly where and when Werbert is?"

"I don't think that will be necessary," a snide and nasally sounding voice that I didn't recognize responded. "Now that you're no longer a threat to me, I think the time has finally come for us to meet again, face-to-face. Hello, McLaron. It's been a long time. Do you remember me?

Perhaps I look a bit different, now that I'm no longer paralyzed by your evil invention!"

P and I whipped our heads around, and saw, hovering right in front of the open doorway of the time machine, none other than Werbert Turmerberm. He looked quite comfortable floating in midair, his legs crossed underneath him while he fanned himself with his notebook, the light stream of steam continuing to pour from the end of his powerful pen.

"Well, hello there, Werbert!" my father cried happily, as he stepped forward and extended his hand to shake. "It's lovely to see you again, my old friend! It's been far too long. Would you care to sing the old college song with me? I still remember all the high harmonies."

Werbert Turmerberm wordlessly pulled out a gun and pointed it at P. I could tell by the look in the madman's eyes that he'd feel no remorse over pulling the trigger, and I immediately hoped my father wouldn't do anything foolish—or at least, not anything *excessively* foolish.

"If you sing that insufferable song or mention anything else about that college, I will make your last moments on earth very painful," Werbert warned. "I have nothing but foul memories of that dreadful place, where you and that smug bandit Doc Holliday transformed my life into a nightmare! I was going to be the greatest dentist who'd ever lived! Don't you see? I was going to be the next Pierre Fauchard! Do you hear me? The next Pierre Fauchard! And then you ruined it!"

"Are you *sure* you don't want to sing the first couple verses of the dental college fight song?" P asked hopefully. "I can start it for you if you like, in case you're feeling a little shy. *Oh, a tooth is a tooth, and that's the truth, but don't forsooth the truth if the tooth is loose, and you can bet your caboose if the tooth is loose that—*"

Werbert fired the gun into the air, causing my father to abruptly cease his singing. I sighed in relief. Werbert was right. It was a pretty bad song.

"What did I tell you, McLaron?" Werbert growled, his eyes glowing with an upsetting combination of rage and insanity. "I told you that I would make you pay for what you did to me, and I have! I told you I would ruin your life, and even though you don't realize it, I have managed to ruin it even worse than I'd originally planned! I have been erasing all of your loved ones from existence, one at a time, while making other terrible changes to your life as well! Just as you saw fit to make terrible changes to my life when you got me kicked out of school and spoiled my reputation in the dental community forever! In return, I have erased your annoying sister-in-law, and erased your lovely wife—I then made sure you were married to the most annoying person in Pitchfork, just for a laugh. Hahaha! I've just now erased Rose Blackwood, your former assistant, who was probably the last person on earth who might have been able to save you from me. And now that I've had my fun, I'm going to erase you, McLaron, as well as your bumbling son, forever!"

"You leave my bumbling son alone!" my father shot back.

"Bumbling? Don't you think that's a bit harsh, P?" I said, feeling slightly hurt. "Sure, sometimes I'm a bit klutzy, and I do suffer from some unusually bad luck, but I don't think that it's accurate to call me bu—"

I was unable to finish my sentence because a duck inexplicably crashed into my face. The duck had been flying through the sky without a care in the world, when it had suddenly made a wrong turn and ended up in the time machine. It hit me hard, stunning me and knocking me to the ground. The duck looked around the time machine, quacked twice in confusion, before spreading its wings and gliding back out in search of its companions.

Werbert Turmerberm looked down at me in disgust, rolling his bitter eyes before jotting something down in his notebook—the plume of smoke pouring from the end of the pen began to darken. The light in the time machine flickered, and there was a shower of sparks that erupted from the ceiling. I heard a deep rumbling noise, which I could feel vibrating throughout my body like a chili supper that wasn't sitting very well. Apparently, Werbert had just done something drastic to me with his special pen, and now I had no choice but to sit there and wait for it to happen. Luckily, I'm quite good at sitting there and waiting for things to happen. It's one of my hidden talents.

"Now, say goodbye, McLaron," Werbert cackled. "I've spent the past twenty years mastering the art of engineering, inventing, and time travel, and I created the most brilliant time-related invention in history, which is capable of doing the impossible, as well as the unbelievable, and even the unthinkable! And now I'm going to use my prized invention, the time eraser, to make you suffer beyond belief! You see, I couldn't think of a better way to destroy an arrogant inventor than by inventing something even more impressive than all of his puny inventions combined, and then using it to rip him from the pages of history forever. I'm going to enjoy watching you fade away, McLaron. In fact, I'm going to enjoy it a lot."

After making a few adjustments to the buttons on his

marvelous pen (which buzzed and gonged like an activated alarm), Werbert quickly jotted something down in his notebook. Another flash of light filled the time machine, briefly blinding us. When my eyes had recovered, I looked over to P. My father was staring in wide-eyed wonder at his body, which was slowly beginning to fade. It began with his hands, but then it quickly spread up his arms like a rash, taking my father away, inch by inch, limb by limb, until there was no more of McLaron Aaron Baron left in existence. As the last of my father disappeared into nothingness, I could hear him softly say:

"I was right. I really hate not existing."

LIKE A HOT KNIFE THROUGH BUTTER

It was down to Werbert Turmerberm and me. For some reason, that seemed to surprise the evil failed dentist.

"What are you still doing here?" he demanded, looking both furious and utterly shocked. "I just erased you from existence, kid. You should have faded away long before your father did. But you're not fading at all. All of you is still here!"

I looked down at my feet, legs, torso, hands, and arms. He was right. They all still appeared to be there. Not an inch of me had faded in the slightest, and I was checking myself pretty thoroughly to be certain. I was in the awkward process of checking the back of my neck for signs of fading when Werbert Turmerberm suddenly reached out and grabbed me forcefully by the wrist.

"What's the matter with you?" he spat, as he knocked me over the head with his notebook and pen. "My time eraser is a perfect invention that has never failed. It is the most sophisticated and clever invention in history! I don't just use it to travel through time, I use it to *change* time, by writing where and when I would like to go, and what I would like to have happen when I get there. Do you understand how incredible that is? I can erase an entire war from history with nothing but a few squiggles of this scientifically modified pen. I can bring back the dinosaurs just with a few doodles. I can make the Dark Ages darker, I can thaw the Ice Age, and I can build Rome in a day, just by applying a tiny bit of special ink to paper! I can do anything with this invention! Look! I wrote, right here in my notebook, that you, Waldo Baron, *were never born*, which means *you cannot exist*. So why haven't you disappeared? Huh? Why are you still here? You're making my incredible invention look very bad, and I don't appreciate that one bit!"

Truthfully, I felt a bit guilty about that. I didn't mean to make the man's invention look bad. I even apologized.

"Sorry, Werbert. I guess I'm just a bit persistent when it comes to existence. It's the only thing I really know how to do. I'm certain if you use your invention—what's it called again, the time eraser?—I'm sure if you use it again on me, I'll fade away nice and quietly."

"You'd better," he warned, as he once again activated the device.

As he did, I dove forward and ripped the gun from his other hand. He hadn't been expecting that. Werbert Turmerberm had assumed that I'd be as daft and cowardly as the W. B. character from those awful books he'd written. Yes, I could be a bit klutzy and cowardly at times, but I was clever and brave when it mattered. Usually. Sometimes. Occasionally. Twice. At least one-and-a-half times.

"Well, well, well," I said as I stepped forward, waggling the gun at Werbert to show him who was in charge. "It looks like the shoe is now on the other foot, if you know what I mean."

"Yes, I do," Werbert Turmerberm replied, as he looked down at my feet. "Did you get dressed in the dark this morning?"

I looked down and realized that my shoes actually *were* on the wrong feet. I do that sometimes, accidentally switching up my left boot with my right boot. Werbert was right; it is what happens when I get dressed in the dark, when I'm not really paying attention to what I'm doing.

What a smart fellow Werbert was. No wonder he learned how to manipulate space and time.

When I leaned down to fix my boots, I accidentally stumbled backward and bonked my head against the control panel of the time machine, inadvertently pressing several buttons, twisting several knobs, flipping two switches, and activating the invention, inexplicably picking a precise time and place for us to travel to. As I did, Werbert Turmerberm slapped his hand against his forehead.

"Now I understand what's happened!" he moaned. "It all makes perfect sense. You are so ridiculously clumsy, that you've actually managed to *fall out of time*. You've tripped and slipped and stumbled and bumbled so often, that the rules of time no longer apply to you. You can't be erased, because as far as time is concerned, you don't exist. Don't you see? You have already fallen off every possible timeline, meaning my time eraser is useless on you. You are literally too clumsy to exist!"

Huh. I suppose that explained a lot.

Before I could respond to Werbert, the thousands of dime-sized lights embedded in the time machine suddenly flared at the same time, creating a palpably hot rainbow of energy, and we began to shoot forward in the time machine, moving faster than ever before. Werbert and

I were thrown backward, and the gun was wrenched free from my grip. It fell out of the time machine and landed somewhere between 1895 and 1907.

All the buttons, switches, and dials I'd accidentally hit had sent the time machine far into the future, and we were headed there fast.

Since the door was still open, both Werbert and I were pressed to the time machine floor by the irresistible force of the winds of time, unable to move more than an inch. I could hear him yelling unpleasant things at me, and so I started yelling unpleasant things back at him, which turned out to be a really bad idea. When the time machine passed through the year 1915, there was an awful loud explosion from somewhere outside, which sent a cloud of dirt and dust into the open doorway of the time machine. The dust got inside my open mouth, and filled it with a terribly gritty and unpleasant flavor. I spat several times, wishing that I had a mint or a piece of chocolate to cover the unpleasant taste.

Which suddenly gave me the earliest stirrings of an idea.

The time machine began to slow down as we reached our unintentional final destination—the year 1965. The *distant* future. I'd traveled pretty far from home in the past, but this had to be a new record for me. I was suddenly farther away from everyone and everything I'd ever known than I'd ever been before. The world outside probably didn't even resemble the world that I had left back in 1892. Everything was likely very different, and confusing, and shiny, and fancy, and futuristic. I pictured a lot of personal flying machines, and other amazing things like horses with mechanical legs, dogs with propellers for tails, and steam powered shoes. I briefly wondered if I could look up my old friend, Shorty, to see how she was doing in the future. I

suppose I could invite her out for supper and ice cream, though she'd probably want to take her grandchildren along with her.

Normally, that random thought of ice cream would have had me drooling like a bear waking up from its hibernation, but not at that moment. Remember what I said before, about how the further you travel in time, the worse you'll feel afterward? Well, that had proven to be devastatingly true. Werbert and I had just traveled over *seventy years* into the future, and the effect was truly horrific. I suddenly felt as though I'd developed full-body arthritis, a detached nose, a shattered scalp, cobbler's shins, turtle flu, total skin failure, happy feet, angry knees, mildly annoyed bowels, a terrible throbbing in my gizzard, and a phantom pain from my nonexistent tail. My brain felt as though it was sloshing around in my skull like a ship caught in a storm, and the ceiling of the time machine looked like it was spinning in circles above me. It was a good thing my stomach was practically empty, otherwise I might have done something rather embarrassing and messy right there on the floor.

"You fool!" Werbert Turmerberm groaned, clearly feeling just as awful as I did, if not worse. "Our bodies aren't meant to travel so far into time, at least not without some proper rest first. You'll kill us both if you keep it up."

"Then undo everything you did to ruin my life," I told him through gritted teeth, as I staggered to my feet, "or I'll keep doing reckless and foolish things, which will likely harm us both in irreparable ways. Trust me. I won't even have to try very hard to do it. Bad things will just happen to us, I promise."

In truth, I couldn't really remember what my life was like prior to Werbert Turmerberm changing it with his brilliant invention. I remembered virtually nothing about my family or my home life. I knew that, logically, I must have had a mother and a father (biologically, it would be slightly difficult for me to exist without having at least one of each) and I vaguely remembered a couple of other people existing in my life as well. But that was all that I could really recall about them, other than the fact that I knew we had all been sent on a mission to stop Werbert, and to prevent him from changing the world with his time eraser invention. So even if I didn't know why I was doing what I was doing, I would continue to do it anyway, if only because . . . well, what else was I supposed to do? I was a boy with no family, no home, and no life, only a mission to complete. I suppose that made me rather dangerous to Werbert. After all, I was a person with nothing to lose, who was immune to his dastardly weapon, and whose lone purpose in life was to defeat him and his evil scheme. Suddenly I felt a little less foolish and helpless, and a little bit more like a genuine hero.

Werbert Turmerberm snarled at me like a camel with a chronic sinus infection as he struggled to bring himself to his feet. The effects of the time travel had weakened us to such a dramatic degree that we both moved as though we were underwater. Once we were standing, Werbert and I began to shuffle as quickly as we could in the same direction. We looked pathetic, like a pair of elderly men with the stomach flu rushing to see who would get to use the outhouse first as we pined after Werbert Turmerberm's time eraser.

The mechanical pen and the notebook had been thrown from our hands as the time machine traveled at an unexpectedly blazing speed, and both items had settled at the lip of the open doorway. Werbert was only a few feet away from the pen when he decided to lunge for it, which proved to be a mistake. Since I was younger and taller, as well as less sore from the time travel, I jumped when he did, fully extending my arms and legs. I reached over Werbert and grabbed the pen a split second before he could, and then I landed right on top of him. He grunted in pain as the full weight of my body came crashing down on him, crushing him like an old accordion. I snatched the notebook with my free hand, and though my body still felt awfully sore and discombobulated, I stood up and taunted Werbert Turmerberm with my happy dance, while dangling his brilliant invention over his head. It might not have been the most mature thing I've ever done, but when you've had a day as terrible as mine, I think you're allowed to be a little bit obnoxious.

"Ha ha ha!" I called as I began my dance. "I've got the pen and the notebook! Now you'll have to change everything back to the way that it was before, or I'll . . . wait, what's that?"

I pointed out of the open doorway at what appeared to be an incredibly large, impossibly heavy, and remarkably constructed flying machine, which was heading right for us.

It was the biggest flying machine I'd ever seen. In fact, it might have been the biggest "thing" I'd ever seen, period. I had only seen one similar flying machine in my life (I couldn't quite remember where or when), but the one that was quickly approaching the time machine was nearly ten times its size. It looked as though it was capable of carrying at least two hundred passengers, and it was soaring through the air at an astonishingly fast speed. The flying machine was painted stark white, with a funny design embossed onto its tailfin, and the entire invention was shaped like a giant metal cylinder with a pointy nose, and a pair of thick metal wings protruding from the sides. I didn't know what I'd expected the future to look like, but I certainly hadn't expected it to look like that.

"I don't know what that thing is," Werbert Turmerberm breathed, as he looked from the giant flying machine, to the notebook and pen in my hand. "But it's coming right for us. Give me the time eraser, and I swear, I'll take us both to safety."

"No," I said, taking several steps back and holding the pen and the notebook high in the air. "I don't trust you. I'll take us to safety. Let me just figure out how to use this thing."

"I should be the one to do it!" Werbert argued. "That's my invention! You'll probably screw it up in the weird way that you screw everything else up. I'm the only person who knows how to properly use the time eraser!"

"You said that all you need to do is use the pen to write down the time, date, and place, and then it'll magically take you there," I told Werbert. "How could I manage to screw that up?"

"I don't know! But you always do! Give me the time eraser!"

"No! I don't trust you!"

"What reason do you have not to trust me? What did I ever do to you?"

"Umm, you ruined my life?"

Werbert leaned toward me and wiggled his brow, smiling in the challenging manner of someone who knows they're holding a winning hand of cards.

"I ruined your life? Prove it. You don't remember anything about your life before this, do you? Let me tell you the truth about your family, kid. Those people who I erased from your life, they didn't care about you. They thought you were a useless and clumsy fool. If you don't believe me, read the Baron books that are scattered across the floor. See how you're depicted in those books? That's how your family saw you, as a mindless jester who cared about nothing but eating ridiculous amounts of food and taking endless naps. You were a joke to them. And not a particularly clever one either."

I looked down at one of the books on the floor. The W. B. on the cover was literally dressed like a jester, and it seemed as though he was trying to eat an entire three-tiered wedding cake *while* sleeping. I would be lying if I said that it looked like he was succeeding . . . I'd forgotten how offensive that particular book cover was.

"Look at where you are, kid," Werbert continued, as he gestured to the blinking lights and the control panel. "You're literally standing in a time machine. A time machine! Do you know how smart a person has to be in order to build something this impressive? You had a family that was clever enough to come up with something like this all on their own! That's how smart they were, so of course they didn't appreciate or respect someone like you. Even if you don't remember your life before this, you can still recognize the fact that you aren't particularly intelligent, and that you don't belong in such a clever and brainy family. Just give me the pen and the notebook, and I promise you I won't harm you. I'll just take us both home, alright? We'll call it a draw."

I looked out of the time machine. The giant white flying machine from 1965 was approaching quickly, and I had no doubt that if we didn't get out of its way within the next thirty seconds, we would no longer need to worry about making decisions about anything.

But Werbert's words had affected me deeply. He was right. I wasn't clever enough to invent something like a time machine. I probably wasn't clever enough to invent something like a functional belt buckle. If my family had invented the time machine we were standing in, then they were obviously much more intelligent than I was. And it made sense that we probably wouldn't find much to talk about—they'd probably be discussing some of the great philosophical questions about life and the general mysteries of existence, while I was busy licking cake batter from a mixing bowl, or tumbling down the stairs, or falling asleep while standing up like a cow. How could we ever relate to one another when we were so different?

"You promise you won't hurt me?" I said to Werbert. "If I give you the pen and the notebook, you swear that you'll save us both?"

Werbert Turmerberm smiled a syrupy smile.

"Cross my heart and hope to die, kid."

The flying machine was getting louder and louder as it approached; the air was screaming from the giant circular engines that I could see mounted onto the wide wings. I began to walk toward Werbert with my hands outstretched, holding out the pen and notepad, and he began to walk toward me, grinning widely as he stuck out one of his hands in anticipation.

Werbert Turmerberm was indeed a very clever man, but he made a mistake that clever people tend to make when they're forced to interact with someone like me—they forget that dunces can occasionally be clever too. You see, I had noticed his other hand reaching into his coat as he walked toward me, and I could tell from the outline in his pocket that he had a small weapon in there, likely a knife or a screwdriver. His intention was to simply take the time eraser from me, and then leave me there to be destroyed by the flying machine in 1965. After all, he couldn't destroy me with his invention, so he'd be forced to destroy me in a more creative manner instead.

When we were only a few feet away from each other, and it looked as though I was about to hand Werbert the notebook, suddenly I turned in the direction of the flying machine, pointed, and screamed. Werbert gasped as he turned to look at the flying machine, and as he did, I quickly jotted down a random time, date, and location into the notebook. Then I grabbed Werbert, wrapping my arms tightly around him, and then jumped out of the time machine. We both screamed as we plunged through the air, rushing down, down, down, until the mechanical pen and notepad went to work, activating the winds of time, and whisking us away to yet another faraway when and where.

Though I wasn't there to witness it, I can assure you that five seconds later, the large white flying machine from

1965 ripped through the floating time machine like a hot knife through butter.

THE GRAND CANYON WAS NO LONGER FILLED TO THE BRIM WITH WATER

Werbert Turmerberm and I somersaulted through time at a blinding pace while we wrestled with one another for control of the time eraser. And as we fought over it, we accidentally made a few changes to the world. It's difficult to argue they were changes for the better. You probably haven't noticed the changes, but that's only because you don't remember what things were like before we changed them. You see, Werbert's time eraser pen is apparently very sensitive, and it will sometimes misread an accidental squiggle on a sheet of paper or on someone's hand as a command to alter time, and so a lot of weird things happened during our struggle.

Due to our fighting, Italy is now shaped like a boot instead of a top hat; there's only one Australia (there's no longer a North and South); cats no longer have horns or forked tongues; The Great Miniature Golf Course of China is now just a Great Wall (sorry); former American President Zachary Taylor is not responsible for inventing the dance sensation "the jibble jabble"; and there are no longer any acceptable words that rhyme with "orange".

So, sorry about all of that, everyone. Particularly about the jibble jabble, which was one of the better dance sensations in history.

Werbert wrestled the pen and the notepad from me several times, quickly changing our direction and taking us to notably violent places and times in history, with the hopes of getting rid of me by startling and frightening me. But I held firmly onto his back, managing to wrestle the pen and notepad back from him time and time again, entering random dates that sounded familiar, with the hopes that we might finally arrive at a time and a place where someone could help me. Our bodies and minds were thrown into chaos by the constant time travel—it eventually became so confusing and exhausting that, for a few crazy hours, we were each convinced that we were really the other person.

"You'll never get away with this, Werbert!" Werbert screamed at me.

"Oh yes, I will, W. B.!" I shouted back. "I'll make you regret ever crossing Werbert Turmerrr . . . er, Turmerber-mer . . . Turmer-whatever my last name is!"

We eventually reached the point where we were both too weak and grumpy to fight any longer. Werbert and I called a temporary truce (we each took hold of the time eraser with our left hand, while we shook each other's right hand to make the truce official), and decided to grab a bite to eat before continuing our battle.

The time eraser had taken us even further into the future, where there were horseless carriages *everywhere*: thousands of large, metal machines teeming down long and complicated stone roads, making loud and obnoxious honking noises as the drivers yelled at one another and made funny hand gestures through their rectangular glass windows. There was noise and commotion and electric lights everywhere—on every horseless carriage, in every building, and even on the strange, blinking signs that were set up all along the stone streets—which looked as though they were advertising unusually white teeth for sale. I heard music playing—loud and thumping music that made my heart race and my feet tingle, though I couldn't understand where any of it was coming from.

It was simultaneously terrifying and awe-inspiring, and both Werbert and I were shocked into silence as we made our way down one of the many stone streets of the loud and electric city, where future people hustled past us like herds of agitated cattle, with their weird and spiked dyed hair (which, come to think of it, looked a bit familiar . . .), and odd little rubber plugs stuck in their ears, and complicated tattoos drawn all over their arms and legs, while dressed in strange and funny outfits, some of which looked like an infant's underpants. Werbert and I got our fair share of odd looks, too, which I didn't really understand. After all, *they* were the future weirdos, not us.

Our search for food didn't take very long. We'd only been walking for a few minutes before *a gigantic hamburger sandwich with a little cowboy hat* stepped in front of us and handed Werbert a glossy sheet of paper. My mouth dropped open as Werbert accepted the paper and began to read.

I couldn't believe it.

At last.

I'd been waiting for this moment for my entire life, and now it was finally here!

This hamburger sandwich man with the cowboy hat was *clearly* a member of an alien race, which I imagined must have arrived on earth sometime after 1965 (maybe the large white flying machine was their space vehicle?). I always knew we weren't alone in the universe, though I must admit to being a bit surprised that the aliens weren't the blue-skinned, bug-eyed, three-fingered monsters that I'd read about in books. In fact, they looked quite peaceful, and also rather delicious. I wondered if there were other alien races in the universe that resembled tasty foods, and if they'd consider it rude if I asked if they ever sampled one another. I don't see how they could resist. I had to restrain myself from plucking a giant pickle slice from the hamburger sandwich man's head.

"For a limited time, it's only five dollars and ninety-nine cents for our *Rompin' Stompin' Cowboy Combo Meal!*" the gigantic hamburger sandwich exclaimed. "That's a quadruple-cheddar, triple-bacon, avocado, fried egg, onion ring, three-pound burger, with a side of extra-large, extra-spicy, cheddar-jalapeño-chili explosion fries, an extra-extra-gut-buster sized chocolate milkshake bucket, and a side order of our signature sixteen fried chicken crispers with eleven different dipping sauces! It's the perfect feast for a cowboy and his young buckaroo. Yee-haw!"

"Thank you for your kindness and respect for my species, Mr. Hamburger Sandwich, sir," I said with a respectful kneel and a bow of my head. "I welcome you and your delicious species to earth, and ask that you have patience with my people, who sometimes act out of fear and anger, even though they usually have good hearts and intentions. I would like twelve of your *Rompin' Stompin' Cowboy Combo Meals*, please. With extra bacon, good sir. And may our respective species share a thousand years of uninterrupted peace. Now, what are these dipping sauces you mentioned?"

"That's not a real hamburger sandwich, you dunce," Werbert said as he nudged me with his shoe. "It's just a man in a costume. Get up and stop kissing his feet. And I don't think we order our food out here. We have to go inside the restaurant. See?"

He pointed to the brightly lit restaurant on the corner, a long and pointy building that was painted in several unique shades of yellow, blue, and red. Someone then pushed through the swinging glass door of the restaurant, and the heavenly aroma of fatty, fried, and greasy food came pouring out, literally making me drool.

"Oh," I said, wiping my chin. "I guess that makes more sense. The future is pretty weird, isn't it, Werbert? Maybe we should put on a couple of hamburger sandwich costumes so we'll fit in better."

Werbert held his index finger up to his lips as he hissed at me to be quiet.

"You can't let anyone know we're from the past, W. B. It could be dangerous. People here would be very interested in acquiring my time eraser invention. In fact, they might even kill for it. If anyone starts asking too many questions, or learns too much about it, we'll have no choice but to erase them."

"Yee-haw?" the hamburger sandwich man repeated.

Werbert glanced at the hamburger sandwich man, whom he'd forgotten was there, and then he turned to me and raised an eyebrow. I nodded my head. Werbert took the time eraser and began to write something in the notebook.

"Hey, what are you—" the hamburger sandwich man began, before his all-beef patty and bun quickly began to fade.

The door to the restaurant beeped as we passed through it, and a nice lady in a grey and red uniform led us to a little booth in the corner. The benches were heavily padded, and made strange squeaky noises as we slid into them. I found myself wincing from the bright lights overhead; everything in the restaurant was oddly bright and shiny and slick, and also somewhat sticky. I picked up the menu, which was the size of a small novel, and began to thumb through the shiny and sticky pages. I was amazed, both at the fact that they had color pictures of all the food printed on the menu, and also from the sheer number of different food options. There must have been fifty different meals you could order, with dozens of different sides, and that wasn't even counting the two pages of delicious looking desserts at the end of the menu. I felt as though I'd some-how stumbled into paradise. I never wanted to leave. The future appeared to be made for people like me.

A pretty woman wearing the grey and red uniform worn by all the restaurant staff skated over to our table and greeted us with a cheery smile and a wink.

"Howdy boys! My name is Barbara, and I'll be taking care of you today. What can I get started for you?"

"I would like this," I told her while pointing to the menu.

"What's that, sweetheart?" she asked, leaning over my shoulder. "The fried chicken tenders? Or the grilled cheese sandwich? Or were you pointing to the chicken fried steak maybe? Or the pot roast?"

"No. I would like everything on the first three pages of the menu, please. And a glass of milk."

Barbara's brow furrowed as the smile disappeared from her face.

"Are you kidding me, kid?" she asked.

I glanced back at the menu and thought for a moment.

"You're right. I also want the stuff on the last three pages as well. But I don't want any spinach in my spinach omelet. Can you stuff it with fried chicken instead?"

Barbara narrowed her eyes at me before turning to Werbert.

"Your son has an odd sense of humor."

"Just ignore him," Werbert said with a sigh. "Bring us two of your deluxe breakfasts, and a cup of coffee for me."

I glared at Werbert as Barbara left to deliver our orders

to the cook.

"I don't need you to order for me, *Werbert*."

"Clearly you do, *W. B.*, because you're going to attract unwanted attention if you insist on stuffing your face like you're planning on hibernating for the winter."

I grumbled to myself, knowing that he was right but also knowing that I wanted a massive amount of food, and that I wanted it right away, and also, sometimes I just enjoy grumbling. Not to brag, but I've been told by my teacher that I grumble at an adult level. And a fellow grumbler back in Newer Oldtown, Nevada once told me that I grumble as good as anyone he'd ever met. It's truly a dying art form, which some of us are trying very hard to keep alive. But does anyone ever say, "thank you" to us grumblers for our hard work? Of course they don't. Grumble, grumble, grumble . . .

Food must be much easier to prepare in the future, because our deluxe breakfasts came out only a few minutes later. Surprisingly, it interrupted a really good conversation between me and Werbert, where he actually opened up to me about his rough and misunderstood childhood. He told me how he'd grown up in a family of shepherds who couldn't comprehend why he'd want to pursue a career fixing teeth. He'd saved his money for years in order to afford dental college, which was why it was so devastating when he found himself kicked out for missing his exams.

"I could have been an amazing dentist," he said with a sigh as he stared out the window. "One of the best."

"As good as Pierre Fauchard, even," I added.

"Maybe even better. Say, you're a pretty good listener, W. B. And I really appreciate that. It's been a long time since I've had someone I could talk to about my feelings. Maybe it's been too long. In fact, I think being on my own for so long might have made me a bit crazy. BAHAHA! WAHAHA! HA-HOO! HOO! HOO!"

According to Werbert, ordering large amounts of food would bring us unwanted attention, but laughing maniacally while strutting across the table like a bowlegged goose was apparently *just fine*. Grumble, grumble, grumble . . .

When Werbert stopped his mad cackling and his silly dance, he sat back down on the bench seat and turned to me with a rather sincere look in his eye.

"Look, I'm sorry I've given you so much trouble. You really aren't to blame for any of my problems, W. B. You're just a kid. I should leave you alone."

"Can we eat our breakfast first?" I asked with a grin. Barbara set our plates in front of us, giving me another awkward look before leaving.

"I'd like that, W. B.," Werbert said with a smile, and then he stuck out his hand. "Friends?"

I smiled as I shook his hand.

"Friends."

See? That's how problems should be resolved between civilized human beings: through polite and considerate conversations. I was proud of Werbert and me, and how our mature resolution had resulted in a wonderful new friendship. Good old Werbert. I could tell that we were going to be the best of pals for years to come.

I turned my attention from my new friend to my breakfast, and I can't even begin tell you how excited I was to stuff it in my face. Though it wasn't the six pages' worth of meals that I'd wanted, it was still a pretty large helping of delicious breakfast foods. There were scrambled eggs, fried potatoes, bacon, sausage, ham, tomato, a short stack of pancakes, and a side of toast with butter. I grabbed the container of maple syrup and began to pour it over my breakfast. Before I was finished, Werbert caught me by the wrist.

"What do you think you're doing?" he asked with a frown.

"Pouring maple syrup on my eggs," I told him, and tried to pull my wrist away.

He looked at me as though I'd just sneezed on his toothbrush.

"Pouring maple syrup on your eggs?" he said, his jaw beginning to clench. "That's the most disgusting thing I've ever heard. One simply does not do such things."

"This one does," I told him as I pointed to myself with my free hand, feeling annoyed that my new friend was already telling me how I could and could not eat my breakfast.

"Maple syrup isn't meant for eggs," he insisted, "it's meant for starchy things like pancakes. You'll make your eggs all sweet and sticky."

I glared at Werbert as I finally pulled my hand free, and then began to pour a large splash of maple syrup all over my eggs, using five times as much as I'd originally wanted, turning my plate into a sweet and savory breakfast soup to prove a point to him. I stuck my spoon into the syrupy mess and shoveled it into my mouth, showing him that he couldn't tell me what to do.

"Mmmmmm," I said as I grinned defiantly at Werbert. "Sweet and sticky eggs."

Werbert started to lecture me again about the proper and improper uses of syrup, so I took a full container of syrup from another table and then poured it all over my bacon, sausage, ham, fried potatoes, and then added a generous sploosh to my glass of ice water.

"Mmmmmm," I said again, as I swigged from my disgusting drink, beginning to feel a bit sick from the overwhelming sweetness. "Delicious. Just how I like my water . . . thick and sticky."

Werbert retched as he knocked my glass out of my hands and then spilled my syrupy plates onto the floor. While I was secretly glad he did that (it's always a bad idea to use syrup for revenge), I was also quite angry, which was why I decided to break our truce. I grabbed the time eraser and quickly jotted down a location, hoping to escape Werbert and trap him in the crazy future—with its bright lights, giant menus, and friendly hamburger sandwich aliens—forever and forever. But as the time eraser began to emit a plume of smoke, he quickly reached out and grabbed me by the arm, and we were once again tumbling through time.

We ended up traveling to a beautiful place in January of 1891, hovering high in the air above a beautiful redwood forest in sunny California. Even though my mind was as scrambled as the eggs I'd covered with a half-gallon of syrup, I somehow recalled being in that forest before, so I wasn't particularly surprised when I looked down and saw myself running down a path. At first, I thought I was simply running after the pretty young lady dressed in black, who was running several yards ahead of me, but then I realized that the two of us were actually running away from a pack of wild pigs. I squinted at the scene and felt more of the memory begin to stir within me. I was beginning to remember not just the event itself, but also the people involved with the event. The young woman in black wore a rose in the band of her hat, and my brain was suddenly jolted by the recollection of who she was, and how I knew her. *Her name was Rose Blackwood.* I took in a deep breath as the memories continued to flow like a ruptured pipe: Rose had tried to kidnap my family, but we learned rather quickly that she was actually a good person, and my parents (*I think that I was beginning to remember them as well!*) had then hired her to be their assistant. Rose was the closest thing I'd ever had to a sister, and as I looked down at

her while wrestling a scientifically modified pen and a notepad from a foul-tempered madman, I couldn't help but smile. I remembered her! I actually remembered someone who'd been erased from existence!

"Rose!" I yelled down to her, though I knew I was too high up for her to hear. Werbert was still squirming on my shoulders, trying to wrestle the time eraser from me. "Up here! It's me, W. B.! Help!"

Rose then slowly lifted her hand, and for a moment I thought she was pointing at me. But when I squinted my eyes to get a better look, I realized she was actually holding up a pistol. I suddenly remembered why she was doing that. She was trying to frighten the wild pigs away with a gunshot, so that they wouldn't stomp me into mulch and then make me an afternoon snack. It was the moment when I knew that she genuinely cared about me and my family, and also, that we genuinely cared about her. It was a beautiful moment in our family history.

Rose then fired her gun into the air, frightening away the wild pigs.

The bullet struck me in the upper arm.

Werbert looked down at Rose Blackwood, and then over at the wound on my arm.

"Well that's a bit ironic, isn't it?"

As I agreed with him, I felt my body slowly going into shock—the fear and pain I'd just felt had begun to paralyze my system. My mind felt as though it was shutting down—I was having difficulty thinking of anything with any clarity. I needed to get down to the ground, so I could get help from Rose Blackwood and . . . and P! And M! I suddenly remembered both of my brilliantly eccentric inventor parents! And all it took was a literal shot to the arm!

"P and M," I gasped, "I need to get down to the Baron Estate! P and M will help me . . ."

Werbert's eyes went wide as he quickly looked down at the Baron Estate.

"I don't know how you did this," he growled. "You've somehow managed to travel back to a time period where Rose and your family still exists! How did you do that? I erased them! I wrote it right here in my notebook, that they would disappear from all existence for all eternity! How did you do it??? How did you find them?"

"I'm very talented," I slurred, suddenly feeling unbearably tired and rather cold as well.

"No, you're not," he spat. "You're a dundering fool!"

"That's true too. I'm foolish and lucky." I agreed, feeling my eyelids begin to droop as I clutched my wound, hoping that I wouldn't feel any more pain in my dreams.

Werbert's expression darkened.

"Goodbye, Waldo Baron," he told me, as he started to write something in his notebook, the top of his pen emitting an even thicker stream of steam. "I'm afraid that our little dance has come to its end. I think I'm going to take you back to the sea, and then I'm going to drop you in the middle of the Pacific Ocean, where there isn't a ship or island for miles. That sounds like quite a fitting conclusion to your story. A burial at sea."

"Sounds good," I murmured, curling up on Werbert's shoulder, trying to use the lapel of his uncomfortable suit jacket as a tiny blanket. "Try not to wake me during the trip."

"You're pathetic," Werbert spat, as his fingertips tightened their grip on the pen. "Did you know that? You're absolutely pathetic. I hated your father, but at least I could respect the fact that he was an exceptionally clever man. You're as dim as a stray dog, and you're as lazy as a potato, and yet, for some reason, I haven't been able to destroy you. That baffles and upsets me."

"So go drop me in the ocean and get rid of me," I responded with a yawn. It must have been the shock from being shot, but I suddenly found myself caring about nothing other than getting some sleep. If I had to be dropped into the middle of the ocean for a few moments of shuteye, then so be it. "Hurl me into the sea, Werbert. Preferably the Red Sea. I'll bet it's red because it's the warmest one."

Werbert's temper (and nostrils) flared. He sneered at me, his eyes wide and his eyebrows arched—and then he exhaled in the manner of an exhausted horse, turning away to indicate that he was through with me and my non-sense. He returned his attention to his writing for a brief moment, but then he stopped again. He looked up at me with one of the most hateful looks I'd ever seen. His per-petually perturbed face portrayed an even more peeved and pointed presentation as he pouted.

"No, that's not good enough for me," he hissed, begin-ning to shake with his rage. "You've embarrassed me, Waldo Baron. And I don't *allow* people to embarrass me. A man named Doc Holliday embarrassed me once, and I changed history to transform him from an American hero into one of the country's most infamous bandits—I also changed his personal history to make sure he was wedded to a woman who was famous for having one of the world's largest noses. Your father embarrassed me as well, and I erased him from existence, after stealing his family from him, one by one. But now the question is what should I do to you? Dropping you into the sea isn't special enough. My punishment to you should be awful, terrible, and completely unexpected."

"How about you change history so I'll be a successful man with a comfy house and an even comfier bed?" I suggested sleepily. "That would be very unexpected. I'm totally not expecting any of that."

"Silence!" he demanded, smacking me atop the head with his pen. "I need to think about how I'm going to make you suffer. Maybe I should slowly lower you into an active volcano, or change history so you'll be responsible for everything terrible that happens in America between the years 1890 and 1980. Maybe I'll make you responsible for the next great war, or for introducing a deadly disease. Or maybe, I'll do something a thousand times worse than any of that, and I'll make you the next—"

I didn't get to hear his final idea because the pointed rooftop of the Baron Estate suddenly struck Werbert right on his backside, knocking me and the time eraser from his clutches. Rose and I from 1891 must have recovered and gotten back into the flying Baron Estate, which, if I was remembering correctly (all my memories were slowly returning, even the ones that I didn't particularly want to return), was now on its way to Chicago for the completion of our race around the country.

The jolt of the Baron Estate had also managed to rouse me from my shock, and I quickly reached into my pocket, pulling out my handkerchief and tying it around my bullet wound. Then I spotted Werbert's pen and notebook at the far end of the rooftop. Stumbling due to the heavy winds and from my weariness, I slowly tottered across the roof of the magnificent flying Baron Estate, coughing as the large billows of steam blew up from our furnace and into my drenched face.

I ducked a flying V of ducks (ducks seemed to have it out for me today—strange, it was usually squirrels and monkeys that tried to ruin my life . . . maybe *all* animals were against me), and then I spotted Werbert edging toward the time eraser as well. He hadn't suffered from a gunshot wound like I had, but he'd been injured by the flying Baron Estate in his own unique way. He waddled like a constipated penguin as he tried to reach the time eraser before I did.

When we were only a few feet away, we both dove for the pen and notebook, but this time, things didn't go in my favor. I was still much taller, and had a longer reach, but Werbert was much cleverer with his second dive. He actually flipped over and landed onto his back, extending his knee and fist so that he could kick me and punch me when I tried to land on top of him, which I did. He knocked the wind from me, and I clutched my aching stomach and chest as Werbert reached out for the pen and notebook, accidentally knocking the notebook over the side of the house!

We watched as the notebook slowly fluttered a thousand feet to the ground, landing somewhere in the large and fertile California forest below. I knew that we wouldn't be able to find that notebook again, not in that dense collection of trees, not even if we had a hundred years and a hundred friends to help us search. That notebook, which contained all of the changes that Werbert had made to the world and to my family, was gone.

"It doesn't matter," he cackled madly as he wiggled the time eraser in my face. "It's the pen that's important, not the book. I can rewrite your tragic ending wherever I like, Waldo. In fact, I might write it directly onto your forehead, tee hee! Wouldn't that be hilarious! I think it would be quite fitting if I were to write the time, date, location, and method of your destruction, right on your face! Hah! Haha! Hahahahahoo!"

He sounded absolutely insane (I've never been a fan of maniacal laughter, and his was particularly maniacal), and I winced and turned away as he leaned over me with the pen, preparing to seal my fate.

Just as he was about to ink me with the time eraser, I suddenly reached into my pocket, and pulled out the heavy item that I'd been lugging around with me for what felt like a hundred years. I slapped it over Werbert's head and quickly fastened the leather strap in the back before he had a moment to react.

It was P's *Open Wide, Stephen*, Device. Werbert had worn it once before, and I have to say that he didn't look particularly excited to be wearing it again. I didn't blame him. Aside from the obvious reasons, it was also a very unattractive fashion accessory. Werbert's eyes bulged out, but he was unable to move any other part of his body, as the old and rusty dental device had paralyzed him. I took out a piece of chocolate (which I'd borrowed from a sweet shop we'd passed in Switzerland during our long and confusing battle through space and time), and stuck it in Werbert's jacket pocket, knowing he'd likely need something sweet to get the foul taste out of his mouth later.

I finally took a moment to get comfortable, sitting on the rooftop and stretching my legs, enjoying the steady pace of the flying Baron Estate as it puttered through the sky, with a silent and mad-eyed Werbert lying motionless beside me. I suddenly remembered that my family was currently celebrating with Rose Blackwood inside the house, as we believed that we were about to win the race around the country. That made me smile. I wasn't usually fond of heights, but I found myself enjoying them immensely as I sat there on top of the Baron Estate, and watched the impossibly blue and open sky up ahead.

When we finally passed a recognizable landmark where Werbert could safely be dropped, I leaned over my father's mortal enemy, and after giving him an apologetic pat on the head, I undid the leather strap of the *Open Wide, Stephen*, Device, and shoved him off the roof. The dental tool came undone in my hand, and Werbert came back to life as he tumbled through the air like a rag doll, screaming as he quickly fell toward one of the most recognizable places in all of Arizona Territory. I looked down to see precisely where he would land with a splash, but then I gasped.

Oops.

It turns out that our battle through time had changed a few more things in history than I'd originally thought.

Namely, that the Grand Canyon was no longer filled to the brim with water.

WHAT A DOPE

Even though my father's mortal enemy had been defeated, I knew that my work wasn't finished yet. I had managed to travel back to a time where my family and Rose existed, but that didn't necessarily mean that when I returned to my present time, they would exist there as well. Werbert had been utterly shocked that Rose and my family were there in 1891 when we arrived at the forest in California, which meant that it should have been impossible. I suppose I had done the impossible by un-erasing them, possibly because (as Werbert had said) I'd literally fallen out of time, or it was possibly due to our time-traveling-battle which changed the face of the world, or maybe it was simply due to my seemingly unending streak of dumb luck. There was also the possibility that it was a combina-

ary of 1891, rolled up my sleeves, and began to write everything I remembered, about M, and P, and Rose, and even Aunt Dorcas. Since I didn't have any paper, I wrote on my forearm. When that forearm was filled up with words, I switched to my other arm—the arm with the bullet wound, which I quickly fixed by using the time eraser to change what had happened. I altered the past so that Rose's bullet actually missed me by a few inches and struck a duck instead, hopefully that same smug duck that whomped me in the face earlier (lousy, smug, whomping ducks . . .). When I filled that arm up with writing as well, I switched to my legs, and then to my stomach, and then my hands and my feet. I wrote about my family's early adventures, and then about our later adventures, as well as the adventures we planned on having in the future when we had finally made some more money. I wrote about flying houses and other flying machines, rocket ships and submarines, shrinking machines and bigging machines, Doppelgänger Devices and horseless carriages, listening devices, time machines, time erasers, outdated dental devices, and more. I wrote down everything I could remember about our lives, and then I got a bit creative and started adding a few other things, tiny little changes to our circumstances which probably wouldn't make that much of a difference in the grand scheme of things.

When I had finished my writing, just as the sun had begun to set on the flying Baron Estate, I found the last bit of bare skin on my body that wasn't covered in writing (just behind my left ear), and wrote the time, date, and location of where I wanted to be.

January 30th, 1892
The Baron Estate

"W. B.! Wake up! We need to be ready to leave in less than an hour!"

My eyes popped open and for a moment I felt practically paralyzed with fear. Where was I? When was I? Was I alright? Did I still exist?

The answers to my questions came quickly as I sat up in bed and looked around. I sighed in relief. According to my calendar, it was Saturday, January 30th, the day of Rose and Buddy's wedding. Everyone in town would be coming to the wedding, and it was going to be quite a party. You see, my father had recently built a huge addition to the Baron

Estate, which he'd paid for with some of the money he'd received for winning an international genius award. The addition to the house was roughly five thousand square feet large, and while he and M typically used that huge space for testing some of their larger and more dangerous inventions, we'd recently discovered that it substituted for a grand ballroom in a pinch. M had used some of the money she'd been awarded for one of her chemistry discoveries (her method for growing fertile gardens in the desert, which was now being used all over the world) to rent several tables, chairs, streamers, and chandeliers to decorate the ballroom, and the best restaurant in Pitchfork had been hired to cater the affair.

I slowly rolled out of bed. My entire body ached like it'd been dragged through the desert by wild horses, but I still grinned when I smelled the heavenly odor of fresh sweets being baked downstairs.

After slipping on my bathrobe, I limped downstairs, where I bumped into Rose Blackwood and my father in the living room. They were putting the final touches on her wedding dress, and though it makes me feel uncomfortable admitting it, I have to say that Rose looked absolutely beautiful. After finishing her veil, P had pulled a small rose from his pocket and pinned it to the front of her dress.

Rose's eyes welled up with tears as she hugged my father, thanking him for everything he'd done for her. My father's eyes welled up with tears as he hugged her back, telling her that he was so happy that she had become a part of our family. And because I was still feeling a bit sleepy and sore, I suppose my eyes might have welled up a bit too. As the three of us stood there with our welly eyes, the kitchen door flung open, and Benedict Blackwood stuck his head out.

"I'm almost done with your wedding cake, sis!" he grunted in his deep and rough voice. "The first two tiers are vanilla, but then the next three are chocolate, strawberry, and butterscotch on top. I hope that's okay?"

"That's perfect, Benedict," Rose said, as she crossed the kitchen and gave her brother a kiss on his stubbly and sun-burned cheek. "I knew that I could count on you."

Benedict blushed as he grumbled into his fist, before shuffling back into the kitchen, his wrist and ankle shackles clattering loudly.

I wore my new suit to the wedding, which I had purchased with my own money. It was a pretty fancy suit: green and blue and checkered, with a long tie and a cape, and a large hat that had an even larger feather poking out from the band. My family had moaned and groaned when they first saw me in the suit, telling me that I looked like a clown. But I didn't care. I liked it, and since they weren't the ones who'd paid for it, they couldn't force me to get rid of it.

They also couldn't force me to get rid of any of the other fancy items I'd bought recently, like my new leather boots, my golden pocket watch, my penny-farthing bicycle, my marble chess set, my new personal library, and the miniature oven and ice box that I'd had installed in my bedroom for late night snacks.

Another explanation is in order, but don't worry. It'll be one of the last.

You see, while I was rewriting our lives (making only the tiniest of changes), I decided to also rewrite the Baron books that Werbert had created, and I credited myself as the author. Our characters were no longer stupid, inept, and unlikable fools—we were now adventurers, inventors, explorers, and crime fighters; people who would do amazing things like travel to the moon and to the center of the earth, battling selfish villains, and saving the country on a biweekly basis. Yes, we still made the occasional mistake (the character of W. B. was notorious for his bumbles), but we always captured the villain at the end, and we always recognized the importance of friends and family. My books had even managed to outsell the Sheriff Hoyt Graham adventure books, which they'd stopped writing as a result.

The real Sheriff Hoyt Graham had recently asked if I would start including him in the Baron books as well—he missed being a hero, and without his books, he said he once again felt like an ordinary nobody.

I told him there was room for everyone in the Baron family adventures.

"W. B.! Over here!" Shorty called, waving to me from the front row.

Though the ballroom was grandly decorated, and everyone was dressed formally, there was no assigned seating at the wedding. Buddy and Rose had insisted that everyone should be able to sit wherever they liked, and with whomever they liked. They eventually had to change that rule a little bit when Mr. Bessie, the crazy old grocer, chose to sit right in the middle of the aisle, but otherwise, everyone was free to be wherever they liked.

My father and mother sat in the front row, looking quite dashing and dapper in their formal clothes: P wore a military jacket he'd been gifted by the King of Sweden, as well as a formal kilt, and a hat that might or might not have belonged to one of his horses. M looked quite beautiful dressed in a gown that'd been given to her by Queen Victoria, and she was also wearing a bejeweled pair of spectacles that P had made for her for their latest anniversary.

My old friend Shorty was seated next to her mother, who wore a formal dress, and on the other side of her was her father, who wore a formal mustache. Shorty was dressed in her typical cowgirl hat, though she had traded in her muddy work shirt and vest for a proper dress. Part of me wanted to mock her for her outfit (don't feel too bad for her; she'd called me by a rather unflattering nickname when we'd first met), but I had to admit that she looked pretty nice. I sat down beside her and mumbled something about her looking pleasant, and I could feel myself blushing beneath my large, feathered cap.

Shorty laughed as she punched me lightly on the knee, causing it to go numb in an instant.

"You're looking redder than a sunburned lobster's

behind, W. B.! I have some great news to share with you! My pa and ma recently decided to build themselves their very own tavern right here in Pitchfork! It turns out they enjoyed their stay so much the last time they were here that they want us to move here permanently!"

That was great news indeed! With all the wonderful success that my family had experienced lately, the one thing that continued to stand out as a misery was my utter failure to make friends. But with Shorty moving to Pitchfork, I'd now have a wonderful friend in town, someone who I knew would always stand up for me. In fact, Shorty proved what a good and valuable friend she was just a few seconds later. There was a kid sitting behind her who I knew from school, and when he spotted me, he made an awful face before reaching out and flicking my ear as hard as he could.

"Hah! Nice suit, Waldo Weirdo!" the boy jeered, chuckling at his witty joke.

Shorty turned to the boy and laughed loudly as well.

"Waldo Weirdo!" she brayed, slapping the boy on the shoulder. "That's pretty darn funny! Hah! That's much funnier than what I call W. B., because of course, it's only okay to call people funny nicknames when they're your friends, and you know you aren't hurting their feelings. Otherwise, it's just mean, and you wouldn't want to be mean, would you? Because I don't particularly like people who are mean."

The boy tried to respond, but he was currently lying on the ground, gasping for breath, trying desperately to recover from one of Shorty's gentle pats.

I smiled at Shorty. She smiled back at me.

The wedding was a wonderful success.

As soon as Miss Katherine and Mr. Dadant began to play the wedding march on their nose harp and washtub, a lovely and veiled Rose Blackwood slowly made her way down the aisle. M, P, Sheriff Graham, and Benedict Blackwood immediately began to cry. Benedict bawled so hard that several of the deputies standing beside him had to reach up and dab away his tears with a handkerchief, since his wrists were still shackled.

Aunt Dorcas wailed and blubbered and boo-hooed until I seriously began to wonder how much water she could store in her eggy body—it was like she was part camel or something. She cried rivers and lakes and oceans onto the jacket of her new friend, a rather unusual looking man by the name of Egbert Florentine. Mr. Florentine was a very nice person, who was always sharply dressed in a top hat and spats—as though he expected to be invited to a fancy ball at any moment. His head was completely bald and slightly peaked at the top, and his body was as round as a medicine ball, which caused him to wibble and wobble as he walked. My family had taken a liking to him right away. Egbert Florentine was absolutely perfect for my Aunt Dorcas in every imaginable way: he was smart and polite, he was clean and well-manicured, he had a good job and a pleasant family, and perhaps most importantly, he was completely deaf.

I have to admit that my eyes grew a bit misty as well, but I didn't cry. Instead, I found my mind beginning to drift toward the fabulous invention that I still had stowed away in my jacket pocket. It was the time eraser, Werbert's steam powered pen capable of changing the world. I hadn't told my parents that I still had it. When they'd asked how I'd defeated Werbert and restored everyone who'd been erased, I had been very vague with my answers. Exceptionally vague. I told them that I had been clumsy and bumbling, and that somehow, after a lot of falls and comedic errors, everything had somehow worked out in the end. They didn't find that difficult to believe. It was sort of what always happened to me during our adventures.

I was purposely vague with my answers because I

had already decided that I wasn't going to share Werbert's invention with them. I didn't want them to know it still existed. It was just too dangerous. I knew my parents were good and kind people, but if they had a device like that in their possession, something that could literally rewrite time, then they would likely be hounded by hordes of people, evil and important people, who would want to use that device for their own selfish purposes. My father had been pleased to hear that his time machine had been smashed to bits, and he had already vowed not to build another one, reasoning that mankind simply wasn't ready for the privilege of time travel yet.

Buddy Graham lifted Rose's veil and looked deeply into her eyes. They smiled at each other warmly.

I had decided to destroy the time eraser, but not before taking it on one final adventure. And I had scheduled my adventure for right after Rose's wedding ceremony, when everyone would be too distracted by the party to notice that I'd disappeared.

Buddy recited his vows to Rose while he slipped a ring onto her finger (P and M had actually made her wedding ring out of a unique metal they'd invented earlier that week, which was resistant to scratches and dents). Rose recited her vows to Buddy next, while she slipped a ring onto his finger as well. Parson Black, who was officiating the ceremony, then presented Buddy and Rose to everyone as man and wife for the first time, and he told Buddy to kiss the bride.

He did. Everyone cheered.

Miss Katherine and Mr. Dadant took up their twangy instruments and started to play as the newlyweds proudly marched back down the aisle, ducking the rice that everyone chucked in their direction. P pressed a button on an invention that he'd hidden in his jacket pocket, and a plethora of multicolored streamers burst from the ceiling, followed by dozens of fluttering doves, which caused everyone to cheer yet again. In the back row, a pair of shabbily dressed men, whom I recognized from one of my adventures, began to sing a rather inappropriate (though admittedly rather sweet) rendition of "Camptown Races."

The party moved outside, where tables and refreshments had been set up throughout M's fruit and vegetable gardens. As everyone took turns approaching the bride and groom to offer their good wishes and congratulations, I quietly slipped back into the Baron Estate. When

I knew that I was alone, I pulled out Werbert's pen, and wrote down a time and place and moment on the palm of my hand. It wasn't very specific, but I was hoping that the power of the pen wouldn't fail me.

THE HAPPIEST MOMENT IN W. B.'S LIFE. WHEREVER. WHENEVER.

After I'd finished writing on my palm, the world around me seemed to flutter like a sheet hanging in the wind, and before I knew it I had taken off, traveling into the future at a great speed.

"Oh shoot," I muttered as I quickly flew from the present, "I forgot to take a piece of wedding cake first. What a dope . . ."

It Was Because of Squirrels

I was beginning to get better at passing through the winds of time. They no longer upset me or nauseated me, or at least, they didn't bother me as much as they had before. It's the sort of thing that takes time to get used to, like riding a bike or balancing on stilts or eating an entire loaf of bread in one sitting.

While it had made me terribly ill in the past, this time I maneuvered my way into the future with ease. Werbert's brilliant invention continued to produce its billows of smoke as it carried me from time and place to time and place as though I was lighter than a feather. As I flew along my timeline, which I admit is sort of like peeking at your birthday presents before you're supposed to, I was astonished by all of the remarkable adventures and wonderful people and breathtaking places that I had waiting for me in my future. It was simultaneously humbling and invigorating, seeing what an incredible life I still had ahead of me. But what was perhaps even more exciting was seeing the great lives that my loved ones had ahead of them as well.

I saw that P would one day be recognized as the greatest inventor of both the nineteenth and twentieth century, surpassing the towering accomplishments of his heroes, Leonardo da Vinci, Archimedes, Isaac Newton, and even Pierre Fauchard. His name and picture would live on forever in science textbooks, which would have been a dream come true for him. He was usually depicted wearing a spiffy hat, while seated on a horse, which was also wearing a spiffy hat. P's horseless carriage, his Air, Oh! Plane, his submarine, and his rocket ship designs would be used as the basis for many of the great inventions of the future—that giant white flying machine that almost crushed me and Werbert in 1965 wouldn't have been possible without my father. Which was good, I guess, though a part of me was still slightly annoyed with him about that.

My mother would one day reach unbelievable levels of success as well, as a chemist, mathematician, and humanitarian. Once her goofy and exhausting son had grown up and left the house, M began to use her talents and generosity to help children all around the world, feeding them with her chemically grown food, finding quick and simple ways to clean their water sources, sending them inflatable shelters, showing them peaceful methods for fending off dangerous animals, and encouraging them to pursue their educations in any way they could. It isn't physically possible to count all of the lives that she had saved with her brilliance and ingenuity. I tried, but I lost count somewhere in the hundred thousands.

I felt like an utter fool for spending the first eleven years of my life searching for heroes in cowboy books, when two of the greatest heroes the world had ever known had been living under the same roof as me all along.

Rose and Buddy Graham would go on to live a long and healthy life together as well. After they were married, they moved into a large home in the middle of Downtown Pitchfork. As expected, when Sheriff Graham retired, Buddy took over as the lawman of Pitchfork. Rose eventually agreed to work with her husband in law enforcement—but not as his deputy. Instead, Rose Blackwood became the first female sheriff in Arizona Territory, a job she performed with pride for over thirty years. She was a tough sheriff but fair, and she had a rather sneaky habit of using clever inventions to solve some of her more difficult and confusing crimes.

After seeing how wonderfully successful and happy my family would become in the future, part of me was tempted to turn back. I had requested that Werbert's invention transport me to my happiest moment of all time, and in a way, it already had. I now knew that my loved ones would all have their wildest dreams come true, which made me happier than I can express through words alone. But before I could change the writing of the pen so I could return to the present and enjoy the rest of Rose's wedding, I suddenly came to a stop.

I couldn't tell what year it was, but judging by all the large buildings and horseless carriages loudly zooming down the street, I assumed I was pretty far into the future, and in the middle of an exceptionally large city.

It was a busy neighborhood that was lined with sky-scrapingly tall buildings, and there was one building in particular that stuck out to me. It was longer and wider than the others, resembling a school of sorts, but it had been brightly painted, like something out of a fair. When I looked up at the sign at the top of the building, it read:

THE MAGNIFICENT BARON FAMILY'S

CLOWN COLLEGE

I stared at the sign, the realization of what it meant

striking me like a bolt of lightning, and then I turned my head and found myself looking over at a grownup version of myself. I was wearing a suit and a hat, though I was disappointed to find that the hat didn't have any kind of fancy feathers in the band. I must have developed bad taste as an adult.

Standing next to the grownup version of me was the woman who I immediately identified as my wife: Iris "Shorty" Baron. Shorty had grown a few inches since I'd last seen her, both in height, and also in the swell of her belly; she was carrying a baby in her arms, and there was clearly another one on the way. I carefully snuck a few steps closer to the pair so I could listen to their conversation.

It doesn't count as eavesdropping if you're listening in on your own conversation.

"We finally did it, W. B.," grownup Shorty said, giving grownup W. B.'s shoulder a squeeze (which made him wince). "Our very own clown college. Now I can teach clowns roping and riding tricks, while you can teach them all how to fall and entertain kids. Hah, did you just hear that? Our daughter, Rosemary Sharon, sounds pretty excited for us as well!"

Little baby Rosemary Sharon then gurgled like little

babies often do. Grownup W. B. laughed as he tickled her little chin, before leaning down and giving Shorty a kiss on top of the head.

"I'm glad she's excited. I hope our baby that's on the way is excited about our new life too."

"I'm certain that he or she will be," grownup Shorty assured grownup W. B. "I know we don't know if it's going to be a boy or a girl yet, but have you given any more thought to a name? I still like the suggestion of naming the baby after your father, regardless of the gender. What do you think?"

Grownup W. B. thought about that for a moment.

"I think it would be nice to name the baby McLaron," he finally said, "but would you mind if I gave it a nickname too?"

Grownup Shorty grinned as she shook her head.

"Of course not. What were you thinking? Wide Butt Junior?"

Grownup me laughed, and so did regular me. Then I realized that I probably shouldn't be caught spying on my future self, so I quickly dove behind a horseless carriage.

"No," the older version of me said to the older version of Shorty as he brought her in for another hug. "I was thinking . . . Smudge. I've always been really fond of the name Smudge Baron."

Since I now knew that there was no shortage of adventure and excitement in my future, I wrote the time and destination of Rose's wedding on my arm, and prepared to travel back in time. I closed my eyes as I was lifted by the winds of time and propelled toward the present, speeding through wars and celebrations and catastrophes and miracles and hurricanes and earthquakes and triumphant victories and devastating losses, experiencing every wonderful and horrible thing that the world has to offer, and feeling genuinely appreciative for the impossibly unique opportunity.

Now, it wouldn't be a W. B. story if I didn't make a stupid mistake.

You might be telling yourself that I've already made several stupid mistakes throughout the course of this story—in fact, I've probably made more stupid mistakes than you can count. But this was a particularly stupid mistake, because I made it not while I was being chased by a villain, or while hanging by my fingertips from a flying house. It was a stupid mistake I made by simply having clumsy hands. While using the time eraser invention, I accidentally wrote down the wrong place, and the wrong year, and I might have accidentally spelled my name wrong too (I can't be the only one who's done that though, right? . . . Right?). I found myself being pulled too far into the past by the winds of time, skipping over my intended destination by miles.

I shot back over two hundred years, finally landing in a big, open yard, right behind a sturdily built house that looked like something out of one of my history books. There was a small boy playing halfheartedly in the yard; he was dressed in funny-looking clothes, with shoes that had large buckles on them. After a moment of staring sadly at a little tree on the border of the yard, he sat down in the grass and started to cry. He looked like a nice kid, and while I knew I should have focused on getting back to Rose's wedding party, I couldn't help but speak to him.

"Hey there," I said to the boy. "Don't cry. What's your name, kid?"

"George," the kid said with a sniff. "George Washington."

"Hi George. I'm W. B. What's wrong?"

George explained to me that he was quite hungry,

and he desperately wanted some of the cherries from his father's prized cherry tree. But he wasn't tall enough to reach any of the juicy cherries at the top. I frowned as I looked up at the tree. I could tell right away that it would be too awkward to climb, especially for someone as clumsy as me. And like George, I was also too short to reach the higher branches that held all the cherries.

Then I happened to spot a hatchet leaning up against the side of the house.

"Wait here, George," I said. "I'll be right back."

Less than a minute later, the two of us were sitting beside the cherry tree that I'd chopped down with three swift whacks, and were feasting on all the delicious cherries we could fit into our mouths. I tried to tell George about some of the great uses people in the future had found for cherries, like cherry soda and cherry ice cream, and even cherry-habanero dipping sauce for chicken crispers. But the kid wasn't particularly interested in any of that. I noticed that George often chewed his cherries whole, pits and all, and I shook my head as I thought about all the damage it must be doing to his poor teeth.

Suddenly, the back door to the house burst open, and a tall man dressed in a wig and breeches stormed out.

"Who did this?" the man demanded, shaking his walking stick at us. "Who chopped down my cherry tree?"

He looked absolutely furious, madder than a tickled hen, and I could sense George quivering in fear beside me. I knew right away what I had to do. I stood up and faced the angry man, looking directly into his eyes with all the calm and maturity I could muster.

"I cannot tell a lie," I said. "George chopped down your cherry tree."

I barely had enough time to activate the time eraser before George smacked me on the head with a cherry branch.

I quickly jotted down a random date and location in order to escape the fury of the cherry-less Washingtons, and after a quick trip along the winds of time, I soon found myself standing in a wide field in the middle of nowhere. I looked around and spotted a barefooted man walking merrily through the dirt, while dropping seeds from a large burlap sack strapped to his shoulder.

"Hi there," I said. "Are you littering?"

The man laughed as he raised his arms over his head

and stretched his back. His face was deeply sunburned, and he looked like he'd been walking for weeks.

"I'm spreading a gift all across this great land of ours. It's important for people to have food wherever they go, no matter where their travels might take them. Which is why I've taken all the seeds from my family's farm, and now I'm planting them throughout our lovely country, walking all the way across the continent with nothing but my knapsack on my back."

"That's pretty nice of you," I said, while not mentioning that it also seemed like an incredibly boring waste of time. "What are you planting? Oranges? Strawberries? Pears?"

"Nope," the man told me, and then he pulled a little green bulb from his pocket. "Brussels sprouts! That's right, brussels sprouts. Every bite is like a mini head of cabbage, only bitterer and smellier, and it gets pretty darned slimy when you try to cook it. By the time I'm finished, this entire country will be absolutely covered in brussels sprouts. *Johnny Brussels Sprouts* they'll call me, savior of the United States. I'll be in all the history books, just me and my sprouts!"

I stared at the bafflingly proud man with one of my eyebrows raised.

"Yeah, about that, Johnny . . . have you ever given any

thought to planting something a bit less gross?"

"What do you mean?" Johnny Brussels Sprouts asked, as he popped a raw brussels sprout into his mouth, wincing as he slowly chewed it. It sounded very hard and unpleasant between his teeth, and speaking of unpleasantness, I would be lying to you if I told you that Johnny's unusual diet hadn't given him a very . . . *unique* smell. If you really want to know what that smell was, I suggest you eat nothing but raw brussels sprouts while walking barefoot across America without ever changing your clothes or bathing. Do that, and then give yourself a sniff when you're somewhere in Idaho.

I reached into my pocket and pulled out an apple that I'd been carrying since breakfast. I looked down at it, and then up at Johnny, who gagged as he forced himself to swallow a particularly unripe sprout.

"Never mind. Great work, Johnny," I told him as I took a large bite of my apple. "I'm sure that history will appreciate what you're doing."

When I'd finished my apple, I turned around and tossed the core over my shoulder, accidentally hitting Johnny in the face with it. Johnny Brussels Sprouts dropped his bag full of seeds as he raised his fist and began to yell at me, but by that point I was already well on my way to another time and another place. I was finally ready to celebrate with my family and friends at Rose's wedding. If I wasn't there by the time they started serving cake, I knew they'd be worried about me. They know that I never miss cake.

I wish I could end the story on that lovely note, but unfortunately, I made another little clumsy mistake. Let's face it. It's what I do. If you haven't figured that out by this point, well, then you're even more W. B.ish than I am. When I wrote down the time and location of Rose's wedding from the present, I accidentally smudged some of the ink, changing the date, so I overshot my intended time in the past by almost twelve years.

I found myself in the grassy area behind the Baron Estate, but there were no chairs, or tables, or food, or streamers set up, so I knew right away that I wasn't at the wedding. I blinked twice, trying to get a sense of what year it was, when suddenly I spotted little baby W. B., dressed in a diaper and a bonnet, crawling through the grass.

"Awww," I said as I quickly ducked behind a tree to watch. "Baby me. How cute."

Little baby W. B. was chasing after a monarch butterfly, reaching out with his pudgy little arms to grab it. Each time the baby was about to catch the butterfly, it spread its wings and flittered away.

I watched the scene for close to a minute, smiling as I considered myself as an infant, marveling at how tiny and innocent I used to be. But then I was struck by a rather disturbing thought. Where were my parents? Why was I alone? I was just a baby, for goodness' sake, crawling around on our property in the middle of the Pitchfork Desert. How could my parents be so irresponsible as to let me crawl throughout nature without a guardian?

I was about to come out of my hiding space and grab poor little baby W. B., lifting him up and assuring him that everything would be okay, when suddenly, a tiny squirrel jumped down from one of M's fruit trees. The furry-tailed squirrel paused after it landed, before slowly turning its tiny little squirrel head over to baby W. B. The tiny creature took a few hesitant steps towards the wide-eyed baby (which was staring at the squirrel in utter bafflement), and then it took a few steps more.

From my hiding place behind the tree, I watched in horror as baby W. B. reached out with his chubby little baby hand, and then the squirrel reached out with its thin and furry little squirrel hand, two baby mammals attempting to make a connection with each other for the first time, and just as the two little creatures were about to touch, the screen door of the Baron Estate burst open, and a very eggy looking woman came thundering out.

"Squirrels!" she shrieked, rushing over and scooping up poor little frightened baby W. B. "Help! Sharon! Help! Your baby has been attacked by squirrels! Vicious, no good, evil, and filthy squirrels! Oh goodness, someone please save this poor sweet child! Squirrels! SQUIRRELS!"

Aunt Dorcas wrapped up the now wailing baby W. B. and quickly ran inside, leaving both me and the squirrel staring after her in astonishment. I opened my mouth and then snapped my fingers, suddenly remembering something that had been bothering me for quite some time.

I had forgotten why I was angry with Aunt Dorcas, but now I remembered.

It was because of squirrels.

No Man Is an Island: Acknowledgments

Thank you to everyone at Amberjack Publishing, particularly Cherrita Lee (who toiled over my scrawl and made it sound pretty), Dayna Anderson and Kayla Church (for taking a chance on me), and Gaby Thomason AKA "Gabor" (who is the best unofficial tour guide in Boise).

I'd also like to thank Agnieszka Grochalska, who I've never met, but who did all of the lovely illustrations for the series.

Also thank you to Curt and Brigitte Bower, who have always been wonderful and supportive, even when I sullied their good name with my nonsense.

Thank you to Hillary and Ryan Pearson and their delightful spawn, Charlotte and Logan.

Finally, I'd like to thank my late brother, Sebastian, who left behind a brilliant spring of wit and insight that I still fish from when my ideas feel dull and flat.

IF FOUND, CALL FOR REWARD

Eric Bower is the author of the Bizarre Baron Inventions series. His current whereabouts are unknown, but since he's rarely needed for things, that's okay.

BRINGING WORDS TO LIFE

Agnieszka Grochalska lives in Warsaw, Poland. She received her MFA in Graphic Arts in 2014. Along the way, she explored traditional painting, printmaking, and sculpting, but eventually dedicated her keen eye and steady hand to drawing precise, detailed art reminiscent of classical storybook illustrations. Her current work is predominantly in digital medium, and has been featured in group exhibitions both in Poland and abroad.

She enjoys travel and cultural exchanges with people from around the world, blending those experiences with the Slavic folklore of her homeland in her works. When she isn't drawing or traveling, you can find her exploring the worlds of fiction in books and story-driven games.

Agnieszka's portfolio can be found at agroshka.com.